Friends Incarnate

Farzana Moon

This book is dedicated to Deb and Phil for their time and patience to edit quite a few of my books, for which I remain grateful. Their honesty and editorial excellence is greatly appreciated.

One ~ In Fetters of Love

A sudden whiff of breeze touched Gable's hair, polishing it with the gold of sunshine from the sky itself, vast and glittering. His gaze was bright but expressed glinting sadness and bewilderment. He was just released from prison, his thoughts intoxicated by the breeze of freedom, yet succumbing to the weight of guilt and loneliness. His cheeks were bony, and his nose chiseled to perfection. The silken gold of a mustache appeared to be quivering, as if he was humming some mournful song.

His thoughts were turning toward the prisoners, voicing this strange epigram that all these men were laboring under the sun to satisfy the lust of spring and its shameless fecundity. *The blades of grass, tall and drunken. Snow-white lilies, naked and seductive. The supple limbs of the old maples hugging amorously. Men tilling and digging graves for fresh saplings, the beads of shame and anguish surfacing on their brows as if to reveal the inner chaos and distortion in their solitary souls.* Gable's mind was still locked inside the solitary cell of his prison, though he was freedom bound, to be welcomed into the arms of his parents outside the prison gates.

I, me, my, these three cankerous bugs inside the garden of one's mind. Illusion and Ignorance, Gable's thoughts were digesting the soma of ideation, sprinkled with the salt of his former antagonism against this world of dualism and absurd-ism? *All of us, so alone and so little in this vast, terrible world of fads and contradictions. Where can one look for a grain of sanity in this sex-crazy, sex-rebellious world of no-sex. Sexist, where even the name of God is haloed by a question mark, male or female, or both?* His mind had left the jail of brick and mortar far behind, but it was tossed into the prison of the material world where liberty and justice were only the phantoms of imagination. The bricks of contemplation in his mind were shattering, as he espied his parents standing not too far away. A sense of elation with all its pain and hope was constricting his heart, his thoughts deflated of all certitude. *Drifting like a white cloud on the faceless horizon of the unknown,* he was swept into the arms of his mother even before he could discipline his aching heart to some semblance of silence and surrender.

"Oh, my son! What have they done to you? You are nothing but a stick. Handsome as ever I must admit but this mustache, how unbecoming." Mrs. Faulkner couldn't take her eyes off her son as her thoughts were filled with both delight and apprehension.

"Don't overwhelm the young heathen with your love and flatteries, Sue." Mr. Faulkner exclaimed suddenly, tossing his head while hugging his son. "He looks peachy to me, and he is longing to get home I am sure." He linked his arm with Gable, dragging him along and away from the hateful compounds of the prison.

This trio scuttled along, talking and laughing in constrained joy sprinkled with artificiality. Gable's hand was reaching for the back door of the white Pinto when Mr. Faulkner giggled like a schoolboy, trying his best to claim his son back with the string of normality.

"Have you forgotten how to drive, son?" Mr. Faulkner cantered toward the front passenger seat to hold open the door for his wife.

"Yes, many things I've forgotten," Gable murmured, sinking down comfortably into the back seat. "Replacing the old ones with the new ones, I guess?"

"We forget and we remember, always clinging to something new as worthless as before." Mr. Faulkner sighed pontifically. "What new ideas or aphorisms have caught your fancy this time?"

"That there is no fear in life, but the fear to live," Gable murmured. "I made friends with a journalist. We shared the same cell," he added, hugging the familiar pain inside the pit of his stomach.

"Another dreamer with no prospect of making a living, just like you." The bitter comment escaped Mr. Faulkner's disciplined restraint.

"He is a successful journalist, or was—"

"Harry," Mrs. Faulkner exclaimed, flashing an accusing look at her husband. "Let's not get into unpleasant arguments." Her voice was pleading.

All fell silent as if a divine command from Above had sealed their lips. The silence was a glacier of ice, numbing the hearts of all three, but the ice in Gable's heart were splintering and crackling. The face of his sister was mirrored in that cracked iciness within. His heart was receiving an onslaught of a recollection that his sister had not visited him even once during the entire five years of his incarceration.

The sun was lowering its shafts into his eyes, blinding his sight and thoughts, the cars on the highway a swirling vortex. His soul was numb and stricken, cowering against the avalanches of despair and loneliness. He could hear his thoughts scream, *So, Maryana has not forgiven me.*

Gable closed his eyes and looked deep into the wounds of his young heart. The ache and hunger gathered like storm clouds. The years rolled into seasons filled with fury and bitterness. Fabian, his best friend, had visited him but twice during those long years of anguish and imprisonment. The queen of his heart, his beloved Ethel, had visited him only once, or was that his imagination. Gable's thoughts were planting doubts while cultivating pain and chaos. *Aslam*, he was recalling, *was visiting Pakistan, probably wooing the houri of his dreams?* One angelic face was emerging forth from the desert of his chaos and that was of his brother Davie. Davie was crippled, the victim of polio, yet ennobled by the purity of his own soul and its suffering.

"How is Davie?" Gable asked.

"He is happy as usual, and longing to see you," Mrs. Faulkner responded as if she had caught this question before it was uttered.

"And Maryana?" Gable's voice was thick with fear.

"She is content. Perfectly happy," Mrs. Faulkner said as her gaze turned to Mr. Faulkner in mute appeal.

"What do you mean, Mom? You sound like as if she is dead? Is she married?"

"In a way, dear." Mrs. Faulkner's voice was barely audible. "To her faith, she says. The convent of St. Teresa is her home now. She has become a nun."

"Sister, Maryana?" A cry of agony escaped Gable's lips. "Choosing cloister as one's grave, while still living? Rejecting life, alienated from the world, oh, merciful God." His heart was bleeding.

"No shame in crying, my son," Mr. Faulkner admonished.

"She is happy, dear. Really happy." Mrs. Faulkner said.

"Happy?" Gable questioned deliriously. "A gentle, sinless soul, my own innocent sister. How can she be happy when she has sacrificed her youth to expiate the sins of her brother?" His voice was choked with self-loathing.

"Don't flatter yourself with such noble presumptions, Gable," Mr. Faulkner chided. "What makes you think that she has joined nunnery to atone for your sins? The sins that you are so proud to carry on your shoulders. No use blaming yourself, or seeking the pleasure of guilt and suffering."

"We are much alike, Dad," Gable cried heedlessly. "I know her more than I know my own self. She loves me. I don't know why, but she does? I was her idol, she trusted me. I broke that trust, and yet she could not hate me for what I did. Why would she suddenly hurl herself into a living tomb?" He couldn't continue, his thoughts beating against the mirror of that awful night when he had killed his grandmother in an act of euthanasia.

"She is living in a world throbbing with the light of purity and that should console us all. Not another word about this." Mr. Faulkner glared into the rearview mirror at his suffering son.

"Not a word," Mrs. Faulkner murmured to herself.

***

A thick curtain of silence enveloped all three once again, and Gable closed his eyes, shutting out the warmth of the sun and the enormity of the buzzing world around him. It was then that the shutters of his memory flung open, gathering that tragic night into their dark arms. The face of his grandmother, wrinkled with age and distorted with pain was emerging forth as an apparition. Infection of the kidneys and years of rheumatism had made her the victim of her own need to die. She cried incessantly, pleading for death.

A pale haze was filling the gap in Gable's memory. He couldn't recognize his grandmother's face, only the piercing blue eyes, much like his father's who had inherited more physical traits from his mother than his other brother and sisters. Those blue eyes were now cutting through him like splinters of ice, drinking in the knowledge of her release from pain through his hands. The night was stormy and her own cries for help were loud but then silenced by Gable's ministrations after he had helped her swallow a large dose of morphine pills, his heart crushed by the blade of gratitude shining in her eyes as if he was her savior. He had saved her from the pain in living, but couldn't free himself from the burden of loss, guilt, and trauma. In a fit of madness and overwhelmed with grief, he had called the police, confessing his sin as to a preacher. Without a protest, he had fallen under the bricks of the law, branded with the scar of murderer.

The haze-mist in Gable's thoughts was dissipating, the pale, restful features of his grandmother were fading into the distance where silence and surcease dwindle to nothingness. The ache and longings were now for his beloved Ethel, the need to touch and hold her into his arms forever and forever. This need inside him was so sudden that he shifted in his seat, his heart pleading for love and nearness. He could feel the whip of his passion wreaking havoc inside his body and soul. Some sort of sickness. A deformity of the spirit so palpitating that he could hear it rising to his throat in a lump of physical nausea. The net of his memories was punctured with the flints of pain, kindling a blaze so swift that nothing could be salvaged from his passion and torment but the mutiny of his need and desire. Nothing was real to him, this precise moment, not even the voice of his mother, coiling through his inward chaos and torment like the serpent of lightning.

"We're almost home." One tender wisp of a consolation escaped Mrs. Faulkner's lips which Gable's inner chaos misinterpreted as the serpent of lightning.

"Yes." Gable was aware of his own laconic response.

"A new home perhaps, where discipline and restraint are to be practiced at all times." Mr. Faulkner breathed stiffly, restraining his own impulse to warn Gable that Ethel had married Fabian.

"Ethel and Fabian are keeping Davie company," Mrs. Faulkner said. "Waiting for you. To welcome you home." Her voice was a tremor of sadness.

The chill of late spring was warmed by the sunshine as Gable trampled over the familiar lawns. His parents were strolling behind while he drifted toward the gleaming wheel-chair cradling Davie. Fabian and Ethel were already on their feet, accosting him with great cheers and happy smiles.

"So good to see you back in this sun-sprinkled home of gnarled oaks and cherry blossoms!" Fabian caught Gable into one warm hug before he could turn to Ethel.

"Thanks." Gable turned his gaze, feasting on the beauty of his beloved beside his friend.

A sudden wave of elation overcame Gable, his arms crushing Ethel to him in one eager embrace even before she could mutter her greetings. His heart was throbbing like a raw wound, but he could feel her stiff, unyielding flesh, as if infused with the currents of chill, fear, even revulsion? Bewildered, he released her slowly, the parched oceans of hunger inside his soul ebbing and churning. He gazed into her eyes, not even noticing that his parents had vanished behind the Gothic façade of their sanctuary of a home. Turning abruptly, he drifted toward Davie where he sat cuddled in his wheelchair. Bending low, he locked his brother into his arms, his heart murmuring some tragic song as if he had just lost something holy and precious, though he couldn't tell what it was.

"So good to have you back, my capricious Saint." A sprinkling of joy and warmth was reaching Gable through the lips of Davie.

"You are a bundle of bones. How thin you have grown?" Gable exclaimed.

"It has been so dull around here without you, Gable," Davie chirped brightly. "I missed you terribly, I must confess."

"With music as your cherished bride, how could you possibly miss anyone?" Gable quipped with his usual bantering tone

"Pull yourself together, Gable. You are neglecting your friends," Davie replied. "Besides, I must capture the light of Herman Hesse's thoughts before it vanishes." He fondled the book in his lap and wheeled away toward his favorite oak tree.

Gable's mirth was truncated. He stood suspended, watching Davie retreat into his own cloister of solitude. So veiled was his awareness that he didn't even notice Fabian and Ethel standing close to him.

"What an odd revelation? Davie can not only see the light of Herman Hesse's words, but could read my dark soul too." Gable's voice was but some vague echo."Not only your brother, Gable, but your friend, too, can read your soul. And it's not as dark as you deem it to be," Fabian commented. "I can even read your thoughts this very moment. You're thinking about Maryana?"

"How could you read my thoughts when they are such a medley of confusion?" Gable whirled on his feet to face Fabian. "Even I don't know what I am thinking about." His gaze alighted on Ethel. One spasm of chilling awareness crossed his brow as if he was looking into the eyes of Maryana, not into Ethel's. "Strange, I never noticed this resemblance before. You look just like Maryana. The same blue, sparkling eyes."

"This description fits Maryana all right. Mine are not sparkling, and not as blue as hers." Ethel said, slipping away toward the table laden with drinks and delicacies. "Would you like a glass of beer?" She appeared to address the emptiness in sunshine, her back turned toward the gentlemen.

"Yes, please," Gable responded.

"I plan to drown myself in beer today in honor of my friend's homecoming," Fabian exclaimed, following Ethel.

Claiming the glass of beer from Ethel, Fabian handed it to Gable and then turned back to fill one for him. Ethel was heaping a plate with cake and nuts, none of them saying a word. Fabian fumbled for the knife, stabbing the apple pie into wedges and slapping one on his plate. Sinking comfortably into the chair beside the table, he set his plate on the side table and began to drain his beer.

"What a great host you are, Fabian," Gable said, setting himself on the chair opposite his friend.

"Host, indeed." Fabian laughed. "Wait 'til you get your own cake and eat it, too."

"I'm designated to serve Davie," Ethel chimed in, holding a glass of beer and a plate laden with fruit and cheese.

"My innocent flower." Gable was easing his way into the familiar mode of conversation from earlier days. Fortunately, the sudden pallor of Fabian was unnoticed by him since he was watching his beloved Ethel, standing there flushed, rather discomfited. "Davie is a saint, if you didn't know. He is a teetotaler and no food touches his lips. His thoughts feed on the light of bliss." He smiled.

"Atrocious as ever, Gable, how brilliantly you mock the virtues of saintliness." Ethel averted her gaze, staring at nothing.

"I can use another glass of beer and I'm famished." Fabian came to Ethel's rescue and turned to Gable with an attempt at banter. "Glad that the prison hasn't robbed you of your intellect. Your wit is still dry as a needle." He returned to his seat, swallowing a draught of beer.

"Feeling the needle-pricks all over, my conscience is stinging," Gable retorted thoughtlessly, his gaze following Ethel as she seated herself beside Fabian.

"Didn't know, you had one? Is this something newly acquired?" Fabian teased, relinquishing the plate back into the hands of his wife.

"Nothing new. That same old bully of a conscience which has the power to brand my sanity with madness. My sinful act of euthanasia was the child of such madness." Gable's eyes were lit up with the fire of memories.

"Euthanasia, my friend, is as remote from sinfulness as light from darkness," Fabian said, his heart aching with guilt and tenderness.

"If only Maryana could believe in the absurdity of your justification?" Gable stole a glance at Ethel who sat there munching on nuts as if lost into the pool of her own quiet contemplations.

"Once you harness the whirlwind of absurdities in your head, Gable, you would notice that you and Maryana are alike. Cold, passionate, and inexorable. Metaphorically and paradoxically." Fabian's soul was hugging the sweet reflection of Maryana in pain and fear. "She has found true happiness in her vocation. We should respect her decision and be a part of her joy and peace." He couldn't continue, noticing the flames of mockery coming alive in Gable's eyes.

"Happiness, a mirage unapproachable." Gable's lips parted in one volley of strident retort. "Gods, religions, and religious institutions succeed in killing one virtue we mortals are capable of possessing and that virtue is the need to love. Sin is the weapon in this charade of piety and godliness, manufactured to torture mankind with this whip of guilt and repentance. Why do we always wallow inside the puddles of our sins inherited or fabricated? Why does one need to absolve oneself of such manmade sin or for the sins of others? Churches or cloisters, all have the reek of false piety, false compassion, the clean odor of conceit and self-righteousness."

"There you have it. I have been telling you about the same thing all along. *Why, what, where,* meaningless words in the academia of theology, much like the sins imagined or contrived." Fabian began with a false sense of euphoria, his heart quivering at the mere thought of disclosing his marriage to Gable. "In this snarling world of greed and wickedness, when one ceases to believe in God, there is no distinction left between vice and virtue. Evil, the sister of goodness, both are sent to exile, and one's own passions waft the scent of inertia and freedom." His attempt at sarcasm was plunging him deeper into the pool of levity and confusion. "There. You have committed no sin, be it in the name of euthanasia, or devoid of all form and reason." His heart was flashing a glimpse of his beloved Maryana, while reflected in the eyes of his friend was the portrait of Ethel, both his possession, both lost to him.

"Why didn't you convince Maryana? You might have saved her from the noose of a nunnery?" Gable pondered aloud. "I adored Maryana, and she worshipped me as if I was an angel. When the knowledge dawned upon her that her angel-brother had murdered her grandmother, her belief in angels was shattered—in me, to be sure. She watched me as a lost soul, I think, taking upon her own self the burden of my salvation by offering herself body and soul to God. What a farce." He paused, his features washed by gentleness as he shifted his attention to Ethel. "My dear, you have not said a word. About my sin, I mean. What is my sentence after my release from the prison, in your opinion?"

"To change the subject, if you wish to hear my opinion." Ethel flushed against the warmth of adoration in his eyes.

"No argument as to this sweet suggestion." Gable beamed. "How is Aslam? He didn't deign to visit me in prison."

"He's married," Ethel offered nervously.

"Married to some houri of the east?" Gable laughed.

"No, our infidel friend married one hag of a heathen." Fabian came to Ethel's rescue, cursing himself inwardly for not disclosing his own marriage and feeling the discomfort of his wife. "He got married to his nurse by some plebian name as Heather. Christians call Muslims infidels, and Muslims think Christians heathen. So, both infidels are joined in holy matrimony and deliciously happy."

"That romantic dolt." The shadows of pain were alighting in Gable's eyes with a quicksilver awakening. "I had the impression he didn't have the guts to defy his family. Those sweet rituals which were so dear to him."

"No need to defy anything. They had a traditional wedding. Heather all dolled up in silks and jewels, not to mention two whole weeks of feasting and celebration. The bridal couple sleeping through their honeymoon, so tired they were." Fabian muttered.

"How very interesting. Please fill me in with all the details," pleaded Gable with the curiosity of a child.

Against the shades of fact and exaggeration and loads of news to share and digest, this trio of friends had not even noticed the lengthening of shadows dissolving into the premature hearth of this evening. Davie was blissfully lost in the jungle of his book, just content that Gable was home and enjoying the company of his friends. The flight of time was unnoticed by him, too, his poetic temperament oblivious to the disk of Sun smoldering so exquisitely in the west in its own flames of citron and crimson.

"Sweet Ethel, my—" Gable's voice was choked inside the flood of his own mirth and Ethel's as he noticed the gleam of a wedding band on her finger.

That circle of gold around her finger was like a brand of fire, blinding Gable's sight, his eyes shifting to another circle of fate on the finger of Fabian. Two brands of fire, quick and searing, had entered the rivers of his very soul, licking and stabbing. Laughter was faded from the eyes of his beloved. Fabian's hand was reaching down to touch Ethel's, two cruel fates mating in circles of gold. Breath was sucked out of Gable's throat, the cry of agony inside him choked and sobbing. The air itself was charged with silence, a hush so palpitating that even Davie lifted his eyes off his book, sadness shining in his gaze in rivulets of pain and sympathy.

"We got married, Gable." Fabian was the first one to splinter this painful vacuum of silence, his face flushed.

"Two precious girls lost in one flash of awareness." Gable began to laugh, the flames of agony and torture from within pouring forth from his eyes and lips. "One, to the empty dreams in a cloister, and the other to sweet dreams inside the cage of wedlock." He checked his mirth and thoughts with the rod of his self-discipline and murmured apologies. "Sorry. Forgive me. My nerves are shattered."

"Gable," Ethel said, and in this one word was all her love, all her sorrow, and all her painful confession. "I was in love with you, I thought. It was a glorious dream as long as it lasted. You were gone, and through suffering came absolution. I must not have loved you, truly and sincerely, that is to say ...." She averted her gaze, unable to say anymore.

"Congratulations. So insensitive and heartless of me." Gable elicited one brave smile, bright and artificial, enveloping both friends in the light of his love.

"You're not upset then. We were so afraid." Fabian breathed relief. "We've planned a dinner party for you. This Saturday. A sort of reunion and celebration both. Old Tom, rambunctious as ever, is coming. Aslam and Heather, of course. And Linda, she can't afford the opportunity of missing a free meal." He seemed to cling to this reed of humor, heaving himself up slowly and thoughtfully. "You will not disappoint us, I'm hoping?"

"I would be disappointed in myself if I didn't join you in these celebrations." Gable lied most charmingly.

"See you on Saturday then." Fabian was assisting Ethel to her feet.

"You're leaving, but Ethel ...." Gable leaped to his feet, as if stung by the duplicity of his own mind, still in shock, still unbelieving. "Of course, she's your wife."

"You're welcome to have a chat with her in private, Gable, if you like. I don't mind and I would wait," Fabian offered, sensing the ocean of emotional vacuum in Gable's eyes and demeanor.

"Thank you. No. Well, goodbye, and wish you all the best." Gable shook hands with Fabian, merely grazing Ethel's before waving farewell.

Gable stood staring into the empty bowl of this evening sky in utter immobility. Davie had wheeled himself closer to where Gable stood as the statue of woe and tragedy, his look feverish and searching the infinite nothingness against the beauty of a sunset so tender and poignant. Gable was oblivious to all, of course, intoxicated by the wine of his pain, shock, and bitterness, the lips of his heart sucking anguish and loneliness from the very flagons of his soul.

"At least, you know now." Davie said, longing to pour the light of his own love into the bruised heart of his brother.

"Why didn't anyone tell me?" One sob of an inquiry ripped through Gable's very soul, it seemed. He turned slowly to face his brother.

"We are either fools, or cowards, or both—all of us, as if you didn't know. For us lowly mortals, these are the greatest of our virtues, we would dare not claim." Davie breathed low, as if clinging to the reeds of profundities to pierce the veil of pain in his brother's eyes. "If we knew how to share the burden of pains within us and with others, as well as to console, we would be the masters of our fates. Not like the sniveling maggots as we are, crawling on the face of this earth with fear in our hearts and with pride on our shoulders. Are we not the victims of our own stupidity and ignorance, letting the needles of our pain lance inner peace and harmony, where parched hungers of the soul plead for a morsel of sanity or wisdom?"

"Your parables, my young Prophet, rise above the waters of average intellect." Gable wrenched his thoughts out of the wild fires of his inner torment, his look sad and smoldering. "How does one silence this hurricane of pain within oneself in this ocean of ignorance, could you tell?"

"Face this hurricane with all the agony of your body and soul, Gable, and it would dissolve. But if you hide it under the veneer of stoic resolve, it would wound and crush the very fabric of your sanity with its own fury and madness." Davie let the quiver of his wisdom and gentleness plunge straight into the heart of his brother. "This is the rite of purification, Gable, and we all go through that consciously or unconsciously, against the incessant blows of grief and tragedy. Let not the pain grow like a canker. Turn it to ashes, consuming it before it consumes you. Talking of pain, I am beginning to suffer the pangs of hunger. We must go in. Mom has planned a great feast, I know, in honor of you, the beloved son." He added with a mingling of humor and sadness.

"Her accursed son, to be precise." A sudden volley of mirth escaped Gable's anguish and bitterness. He stirred to his feet, aiming straight for the white pillars smothered in ivy, the red geraniums on the porch staring back at him from their own muddied graves.

This untimely death of something precious in Gable. I was afraid of that, Davie thought. The pain of love churning inside him was much like the crunching of wheels on his wheelchair as he followed Gable.

Two ~ Symphony of Pain

The rills of moonlight dancing through the window in Gable's bedroom were caressing his wearied form sprawled on the great bed. After the night of great feasting with his family, he had abandoned himself upon his bed fully dressed, unable to move or think. The taste of dinner was still in his mouth and the reflection of all details with their bright incongruity were his companions with sleep and loneliness. Pain was his companion supreme, drugging him with its wine of agonies both aged and sparkling. The vast dining room with its teardrop chandelier was suspended inside the haze of his dreams like some old and terrible memory. In the background was the pale dusk streaming through the French doors much like the mists in thoughts and fantasies. Hovering above and below were the clouds in voices and expressions, the imponderables. The naked, unashamed light of *understanding* in Davie's eyes and the tender, loving protectiveness of his parents were also there. All so precious, all so unutterable, all so heartrending.

The night was bright and silent, much like Gable's soul, and he would have been able to feel the aching resemblance between the two had he been awake. His dreams were shifting from the ache of silence to the music of elation. *Some sort of euphoria where hopes and desires merge and dance, creating one shuddering ripple into the vacuum of nothingness. An eternal and beautiful mirage. Not a mirage, but a shrine of love, sanctified by the hymn of one name alone, Ethel? Ethel was with him, their lips tasting the soma of bliss, and their souls transported to the sublime purity of a paradise where the blooms of love were sweet and everlasting.*

The voice of his psyche was a distant murmur in the background, humming to him secrets dark and profane. *If he was to live that dream a million times over, he would long for sleep all his blessed life, welcoming death, if not Judgment Day?* He could hear one clap of a thunder in his soul, the rod of lightning pouring down a merciful shower of rain and illuminating the garden of his youth. The carefree, mindless days were wet and slippery, he could see himself rolling over the lawns, or chasing Maryana. The face of his grandmother was emerging forth like a white cloud, twisted with pain and parched with the longing of death.

So many shades and visions were swallowed by the greed of the hungry night. The hours, too, were fading and awakening into the mouth of a dawn. Gable's eyes were fluttering open in obedience to the command of the light, his pallor attaining a subtle blush against the morning haze streaming through his window in dreamy rivulets of gold and crimson. He eased himself up slowly and painfully, each muscle in his body aching and protesting. If that was not enough, he could hear his soul uttering groans and weeping inconsolably. He was startled to his feet, chilled to one spot by the rude intensity of his own reflection in the mirror on his dressing table. It was the reflection of a man unkempt and haggard, his pallor as dull as the thatch of pale gold on his head, all limp and disheveled. His eyes were swollen and red-rimmed; lowering fires down his golden mustache to his lips the color of blood. Whirling away from this stranger in the mirror, he drifted toward his writing desk. Letting his fingers feel the cherry finish, he stooped over the neatly piled books as if longing to devour them whole. A stab of pain, sharp as a sword's cut, was spiraling up his back from the wounded depths in his soul. He staggered away, intending to wash all pain under the violence of a cold shower.

The light of dawn was a silent murmur of pain in Gable's eyes as he stood dressed and groomed by his bedroom window, overlooking the neat lawns, all gold and emerald against the flood of sunshine. Mute pain and bitterness were his morning companions and his heart felt empty of all emotions. Turning away abruptly, he sprinted toward the staircase. Inside him was hunger, hunger of the soul unfed and of the spirit in utter neglect. He bustled forth into the dining room. He was quick to wish his parents good morning at the table, bestowing a charming smile at the maid, whom he remembered as Caroline.

"What's for breakfast, Mom? It seems like I haven't eaten for a year," Gable said cheerfully.

"Your favorite blueberry muffins. Cheese omelet, Caroline's special favor to you. And coffee, of course." Mrs. Faulkner smiled.

"What are your plans for today, son? Doing anything?" Mr. Faulkner asked, pretending to read the newspaper.

"Nothing." Was Gable's noncommittal response as he dabbed his blueberry muffin with butter.

"Quite an onerous enterprise, this *nothing*." Mr. Faulkner's gaze was a flood of disapproval. "Writing something, no matter how worthless, even the contemplations of a prisoner, is better than sheer indolence. This simple occupation can lead one to stardom, I have heard …." His thoughts were truncated as he encountered a sudden blaze of pain in the eyes of his wife.

"Harry." Mrs. Faulkner's very protest was charged with reproof.

"Mother." Gable murmured a soft appeal, pouring himself a cup of coffee.

"Mr. Dern would help you pick up the threads of the old trade, writing, as you call it." Mr. Faulkner breathed assertively, recovering his sense of authority and ignoring the odor of constraint. "He's the owner of a biweekly, running ten thousand copies at the most. You would be of a great benefit to him; besides earning a little, just to write an article or two in a month."

"I can't write one decent sentence, Dad, not yet anyway," Gable protested. "I can barely scribble, and the desire to write is no more. If I do recover from this inertia or writer's block, I might turn out to be a mediocre writer. To think of it though, unskilled as I am in other fields, mediocrity may be my only means of salvation, if not sustenance." He opined aloud, chewing on his muffin as if it was a hard biscuit.

"Here, have a fresh cup of coffee, Harry," Mrs. Faulkner offered, her eyes still glinting reproof at her husband.

"No, thank you, dear," Mr. Faulkner said, his look contemplative as he shifted his attention back to his son. "Mediocrity is gold in this world of greed and technology, where imbeciles make as much as millions, and witless fools laugh up their sleeves while hoarding treasures stolen from the coffers of the poor. You would be as successful in your mediocrity as any numbskull boasting of talent or intellect." His eyes were holding the blades of rectitude, aimed to rip open the false equanimity of his son. "You must never belittle your own intelligence, and Mr. Dern is the man to lend you inspiration," he added.

"A few pieces of disjointed prose and poetry published in insignificant journals don't really give me any ammunition for success, Dad." Gable attacked the plate of omelet with passion. "If you wish to accommodate a striving author with the promise of food, shelter and clothing, I would try my best to endure the pangs of failure without a protest. I could start right after breakfast, staring at the blank page if nothing else. If that fails, I could do windows, a grand exercise to fight the writer's block. I am almost forgetting. First, I must see Maryana."

"Sister Maryana, you mean." Mr. Faulkner succeeded in eliciting one twig of humor, noticing the defiance in his son's eyes.

"I mean, my sister, Dad," Gable responded sullenly

"No point in quibbling over the name, dear," Mrs. Faulkner interceded, her voice gentle and spilling endearments. "Maryana can receive visitors between two and four in the afternoon," she said.

"Visitors. I am her brother." A mad, senseless hysteria escaped his lips.

"No streaks of dementia or insanity run in our family, I am sure." Mr. Faulkner uttered. "Control your moods, Gable, or you would end up in the hothouse of idiots and imbeciles." His own restraint was running ragged.

"If you have nothing pleasant to say to your son, Harry, keep your judgments to yourself." Mrs. Faulkner couldn't hold back to defend her son.

"These are not judgments, dear, but harsh realities." Mr. Faulkner heaved himself up slowly and thoughtfully. "At least one week of rest is recommended to calm your nerves, son, that's my advice." Planting a hasty kiss on his wife's cheek, he bolted for the door. "A whole day's work and then mandatory meeting in the evening. Won't be home for dinner." He tossed this bit of information over his shoulders before stepping out into the flood of sunshine.

While Gable sat brooding at the dining table under the soliciting gaze of his mother, Mr. Faulkner was plodding toward his car under the familiar burden of despair growing inside him like an ulcer. The white shadow of his own soul was hovering above, revealing to him the mirror-image of his own self inside the youth of Gable. He was young again, wild and invulnerable. He deemed this entire world an ocean of greed and selfishness, a craven and merciless world where each person was either a tyrant or a hypocrite. His thoughts were whirling with the speed of a rocket inhaling the reek of humanity, its vices and virtues. The steering wheel was cold under his hot hands, and he was wooing his sanity with the vision of his son seated beside his mother, docile and ingratiating. Had he known the efficacy of his vision, he would have turned back, reclaiming love and laughter.

"Sorry, Mom," Gable said. "You are so kind and loving. And this brute of a son ends up hurting you, unintentionally, of course."

"How foolish you are, Gable. You are my joy and sunshine." Mrs. Faulkner smiled, as she got to her feet.

"Love you, Mom, you know that." Gable kicked back his chair and quickly stood. "A morning walk would mend my nerves. Maybe dad is right." He sauntered out of the room, sober and ponderous.

The chill in the morning air sent a sting of pain through Gable's veins as he emerged out on the porch. All the silent pain of the night before came marching into his head. He almost staggered under this brutal, stabbing assault of awareness that his one and only beloved, Ethel, was lost to him. His world was welcoming not sunshine, but despair and hopelessness. Finding himself in his backyard with elms and cedars hovering above him like the sentinels of fate, he abandoned himself on the white swing. A patch of daisies huddled together under the glare of the sun were attracting his attention, but he closed his eyes, feeling only the hopelessness from within. The scent of lilacs from behind was teasing his senses, and he could literally taste the whiff of pain and nostalgia, Ethel sitting beside him and laughing with a carefree abandon. The icy blue in his gaze was a torch of pain as he forced open his eyes, overwhelmed by the sudden weight of loneliness.

How quiet and peaceful it is here, and yet it's all an illusion. Nature itself guarding its river of torment against its façade of tranquility. In this world of conceit and selfishness, it doesn't matter how truly one loves, but how utterly one succeeds in deceiving. What brings us together as friends is not the scent of virtue in our hearts, but the reek of mendacity in our minds, which we love and understand with perfect candor from within and without. His thoughts were jolted out of their dark reveries by the sudden unfolding of a symphony in the air.

The notes of the last symphony by Beethoven were coming alive under the magical touch of Davie's fingers. Gable's soul longed to absorb the ebb and flow of this divine melody. Heaving himself up, he drifted back toward the house, oblivious to the purity of warmth and sunshine. His heart itself was a symphony of which tore through his breast like a blade of ice. He was driven toward the music like the one longing for self-annihilation. Entering the parlor unnoticed, he abandoned himself on the sofa, his gaze slipping from his brother's back to his lifeless legs. The wildfire of his own agony was dissipating, finding consolation in the rhythm of Davie's genius as he began to strike the tunes of his own inspiration. Gable's soul was constricting and expanding, almost stumbling towards the rungs of exaltation, before the music came to an abrupt halt with a terrible scream, much like the cry of torture.

"Such brutal slaughtering of music, Davie. What possessed you to kill it thus?" Gable exclaimed involuntarily.

"A flattering comment indeed." Davie spun his wheel-chair around to face his brother. "I would have played divinely had I been aware of the privilege of an audience." Poetic mirth flashed in his eyes.

"You don't need audience, Davie." Gable's own sense of poetry and imagination was breaking loose from the ocean of his inner torment. "Your music has the power to create a hall full of audience, absorbing each note with a hush so stark that no thunder of applause could ever match their silent praise and reverence."

"What a pity, Gable that you are trying to hide your pain against the façade of fake epigrams." Davie smiled. "Why not be brave and spill it all out? One can live with the physical deformities, but the mental ones are difficult to endure. You have lost—not only love, but faith, in God, it seems."

"You would be good in preaching sermons if not in delivering distortions." Gable chuckled under the burden of some narcotic sense of pleasure. "You, of course, would never lose faith in your god, be he Bacchus or Dionysus, for music is the nectar of your life, the very breath of living, and you loving it, rather worshipping. As for me, the pain of my loss is no larger than this cosmic struggle in living, suffering, and stumbling over the waves of sin and penance."

"Is it guilt, Gable, larger than pain and love, rising above your loss in a fever of stoic indifference?" Davie challenged, bent on probing the tortured deeps in his brother's soul and psyche.

"Guilt is the reward of wrongdoing, Davie, and I don't consider my actions wrong in relieving the sufferings of Grandma. If faced with the problem of sin and morality once again, I would behave the same as I did before, free of guilt or blame." Gable was donning the mask of profundity to veil his inner torment.

"In God's name, Gable, one must learn to respect the laws of this world or perish," Davie exclaimed.

"God as my witness, I dare not tell lies. I have not lost faith in God as you presume. God as my guide, I seek His mercy. And this very process of *seeking* has lent me a little understanding that the most merciful of gods is the God of death." His vehemence was truncated by the sudden arrival of Davie's piano teacher.

The afternoon hours in trivia of tragedies past and recent were slithering past in conformity with Gable's pacing in his bedroom as if competing in a marathon of madness. After murmuring a stiff greeting with Mr. Preston, Davie's piano teacher, Gable had sought the sanctuary of his bedroom. Forcing himself to sit at his desk with a blank paper staring at him, he had tried to discipline his thoughts. His thoughts had strived toward projecting words on the paper, which he could neither write, nor forget. Abandoning this task as utterly impossible, he had begun to pace, his mind empty. He was floating, rather than pacing inside clouds of fogs and mists where reality couldn't be seen, and illusion itself blackened by the soot of timelessness. His spirit was lost and inconsolable, pleading with Ethel to come back, and foundering inside the murky waters of his own love and disconsolation. Another plea was escaping his heart willing its appeal to reach Maryana in an effort to snatch her away from the cloister of absurdities.

Somewhere out there was the *moon* of his agony, his love incarnate, the Venus of his loss, his beloved Ethel. The sun of his torment was obscuring all, hurling forth another constellation, the *star of grief*, in the semblance of Maryana. She was conspiring with the vestal virgins of Rome and wearing the smile of a pagan Princess. A cry of supplication was in the air, an echo most terrible from the chaos within his soul and psyche. The *moon of agony* was colliding with the *star of his grief*. Time itself was sounding its forlorn call from the prison of a clock on the mantelpiece. Gable's feet were heeding this call, coming to a sudden halt with one jolt of awareness and digging deep into the Aubbuson rug with the weight of lead. Standing still like the one stricken, his thoughts, too, were relenting and seeking the stillness. Skilled as he was in divorcing all pain with one convulsion of a smile, he breathed deep and emerged out of his room calm and victorious. Cantering down the spiral staircase, he landed straight into the dining room where his mother stood admiring her own floral arrangement of fresh flowers.

"Never thought I would be ever anxious or apprehensive to see my own sister? I am ready if you are, mother?" Gable bustled closer, smiling winsomely.

"How do you like my flower arrangement?" Mrs. Faulkner turned around dreamily, facing her son.

"Splendid, Mom. Beautiful," Gable complimented, snatching crimson from the roses as a balm to his own wounds. "Should we be going?"

"Sorry, Gable, didn't I tell you?" Mrs. Faulkner replied with great consternation. "Christina, your garrulous aunt called to announce that she would be here this afternoon. I better stay, or she would rave and complain. You know how she is? Won't you postpone?"

"I wish …." Gable's mask of repose was threatening a breakdown. "Is she really my aunt? I mean, really, your sister? How she tries my patience? But don't worry, Mom, I would behave most charmingly when I get back." He fled abruptly.

Mrs. Faulkner was numb and speechless. She was caught in abeyance as if whipped by the rod of a revelation. Her soul was reflecting the souls of her own deformed and crippled children. But one soul was asserting its light of purity and wholeness, and that was Davie's.

Three ~ Sister Maryana

The bare walls of the nunnery in the spacious vestibule were reflecting sunshine as Gable stood looking out of the rectangular windows while waiting for Maryana. Turning with a sudden abruptness, he began to pace, noticing two armless chairs and a vesperal stand that were dull and unwelcoming. A painting of The Last Supper huddled over the imposing doors in the distance was gathering more colors from the light reflected through the stained-glass window, almost making it alive. Gable retraced his steps. He was drifting toward the naked windows, sunlight blinding his eyes, as if he had just noticed it, or as if it had appeared magically to sting his eyes with its shafts of gold and haze. This sudden sting was carving its way down the sanctuary of his inner abyss and silence as his feet came to an abrupt halt by the east window.

Maryana is much like me, wild and untamed? A perfect stranger to her own whim and caprice. Crushed by the shadows of poetry and imagination. Gable's thoughts were chilled by the echo of tenderness, so near, so dear.

"Gable, Gable." Maryana was seeking his attention in a prayer-like supplication.

"Maryana." Gable swung around, snatching her to him in one eager embrace. "Let me look at you." He cupped her pale cheeks into his trembling hands. "So sad and beautiful." He said, her white habit suffocating his thoughts.

"Foolish as ever, my poet Brother," Maryana chanted. "That look in your eyes, Gable? Do we know each other? This is not the first or the last time that we see each other." She was trying to fathom the blue deeps in his icy gaze.

"Hope not," Gable said. "What in the name of absurdity made you choose the nunnery? You will suffer, my dear, suffer terribly. Much like me, you are driven by your whims. The rivers of love inside you cannot be quenched with chastity and prayers. Such miserable creatures as we are we cannot love God alone!"

"I am sorry you feel that way, Gable. We are strangers, after all." Maryana uttered.

"No, Maryana, we are not strangers. I can see your mind and soul with as much clarity as I can my own. These vestal garments are not going to protect your soul from aching and hurting, and hungering for something more than piety and renunciation. This is a living death, Maryana, and I am not going to let you die. Come home with me, you must." His tirade was more of a plea than a warning.

"I cannot, Gable, I can't. I have taken a vow." Maryana said hopelessly.

"Why, Maryana, why did you do it?" Gable's eyes were lit with the fire of inner torment. "You cannot deceive me. I want to hear the truth."

"Could you tell if lies escaped the lips of a nun?" Maryana ventured a stab at humor. "I don't know, Gable, honestly I don't. Maybe you are right. I am the prisoner of my own moods, as you are. We are fated to suffer, both of us." The dreamy look in her eyes was kindling the lamps of recollection. "There's a streak of madness in our family, though Dad doesn't believe so. Davie may appear immune to such madness, but he is afflicted just the same. Mom is the only one, the queen of sanity. Remember how we studied Pascal, Spinoza, Descartes together, comparing notes? Trying so very hard to fill the vacuums of our ignorance with arguments. Our hearts empty and our minds brimming with ideas, and our souls searching for something but not knowing what. We were getting nowhere, and then, grandma. You were in prison and then Fabian …." A hot flush pervaded her cheeks at the mere mention of Fabian. "I had no choice, grief and madness, yes. Sorry, Gable, I shouldn't be talking about … you are suffering, forgive me." She was trying to wrench herself free from her own tortures of love for Fabian, whom she thought she had forgotten.

"My sufferings, can I dare deny to you?" A bitter string of mirth snapped through Gable's lips. "Mad and besotted I am, I know. Thinking, that you chose nunnery to atone for my sin. The irony of fates, we both lost love and faith in our mad quest for something greater than mystery and madness. You will not find peace here, Maryana. You cannot flee from pain and loss. Come home." His tone was tender and pleading.

"I cannot, Gable, believe me. This is my home. Madness has left me." Maryana said.

"Yes." One echo of his own hopelessness was Gable's response.

"How brave you are, Gable. Must be a terrible shock to know that Ethel is married?"

"Twice as terrible since I lost my sister, too." Pain and delirium were shining in Gable's eyes. "I am not as brave as you presume. This pain of losing Ethel will stay with me forever. Can't stop loving her. Wish, I can forget. Some imbecile hope inside me keeps churning, but I can't talk about it. Miss seeing you at home, Maryana, miss you terribly. Have you found peace here, if not salvation?" He asked abruptly.

"Both." Maryana elicited one bright smile while her heart shuddered under the burden of this lie as if she had desecrated the purity of this whole sanctuary.

"You are in love, Maryana, intoxicated by God. Is it possible?" Gable noticed the luminescent blue in her eyes. "Can't imagine my sister being possessed by some love divine," he opined aloud, puzzled by the sudden flush on her pale cheeks.

"Love and peace. Who could not feel these in this abbey?" Maryana was jolted out of her pain and reverie by the sudden tinkling of bells. "How sweet are such sounds? They are calling nuns to the vespers. I must go." She held out her hands.

"So, the heathen is dismissed." Gable held her into his arms in one delirious embrace, planting a hasty kiss on her brow. "I will return to my own scaffold of life. Pray for me, Maryana." He stood gazing into her eyes.

"All my prayers are just for you, Gable," Maryana said.

"When will you visit us?" Gable asked hoarsely, overwhelmed by this sudden sense of loss and loneliness.

"Soon, I promise." Maryana averted her gaze.

"Bye. I will be waiting." Gable turned abruptly and plodded away, his heart empty.

Maryana stood motionless, watching her brother leave as if dreaming a dream. Her heart was heavy, sobbing and weeping in its own depths of silence. Her legs were weak and trembling as a hurricane of desires inside her churned and wreaked havoc. Passions were consuming her sanity, the face of her brother lost and obliterated. Instead another face was emerging forth before her sightless eyes, both angelic and unapproachable. And yet, this was the face of a Lucifer, holding the lamps of love and adoration in his eyes and corrupting her heart with temptations.

I dare not attend the vespers when my heart is burning in the fires of hell. One sob of a prayer was torn out of Maryana's soul as she lumbered toward the sanctuary.

As if carried on the clouds of fate, Maryana was drifting not toward the sanctuary, but out into the solitude of a small garden, her own prison and retreat. Abandoning herself on the wooden bench, she covered her eyes with her small, white hands, as if shutting off the vision of her beloved no other than Reverend Valenty himself. If ache and longing were the fire in her soul, then shame and mortification were pounding her head with the mortars of agony. Somewhere out there was the reflection of her first love, Fabian. In this reflection was forged the tragedy of her silence. She had not ever dared confess her love to Fabian. The mists all gossamer and painful were revealing her madness, as she sat there drenched in her misery, her eyes shielded and her body shivering under her white habit. Void and blackness were clearing the mists, greeting chaos and confusion. Gable was in prison. Fabian and Ethel were married. She herself was buried under the rocks of despair and hopelessness. Her silent love for Fabian had attained the fury of a storm, and she was numb with pain, stricken and annihilated. Paralyzed with fear and agony, she had stumbled into the fetters of a nunnery.

God. With this one word in the silent abyss of her soul contained all her love, all her agony, all her suffering.

Maryana was chilled inside her suffering as the one galvanized. Out of the cold, stabbing pools of Reverend Valenty's eyes were shooting forth the stars. She was the victim of *tragedy* and *timelessness*, melting under his gaze. Her eyes were stinging with tears. Sorrow and madness were her companions, flitting in and out like the phantoms of the night. Gable was her *idol*, broken and desecrated. Fabian was her beloved, lost and forsaken. Reverend Valenty was her Savior, godlike and irresistible. She was sinking deeper and deeper into the rivers of her own pain and convulsion until she heard the beloved voice, the daggers of reality cutting her bosom into lumps of pain and deformity.

"You are crying again, my child, why?" Reverend Valenty pressed her hands into his own. The hazel pools in his eyes spilling the nectar of love and worship.

Stunned and speechless, Maryana was caught into one loving embrace, the lips of Reverend Valenty crushing hers with the violence of a man possessed and drowning. Fragrance and sunshine were seething inside her in an ocean of bliss, but before she could gather the scent of ecstasy, the *divine lover* had torn himself away, fleeing.

Four ~ Phantom of Dreams

The longed-for Saturday with the prospect of seeing Ethel was finally here, after eons of wait, Gable was thinking, while pacing in his room under some spell of fever and delirium in thoughts. The confetti of gold sunshine was pouring in through the window, but he seemed oblivious to the beauty of this day with all its promise of joy and warmth. Ethel was the goddess of tyranny in his thoughts, reigning supreme and carving her way down to the throne of his soul where it lay bleeding, lacerated.

The story of my life. If I can write it the way I want it to be? Gable's thoughts were wandering over to the stack of papers on his desk, awaiting his whim or indulgence.

Gable was assigned to critique an article written by Bryan and had promised his Publisher that this would be done overnight, if not during the day. The article was long, and finding it dull, he had begun to pace with the intention of returning to it soon. But it still lay there neglected, and Gable's pacing was nowhere closer to resting, or curling up under the cherry desk for comfort. Ethel was with him like the phantom of dreams. He couldn't see her, his sight longing for a glimpse of that beloved face, his senses aching for the music of her voice, and his heart drumming tunes harsh and mournful. A sudden revelation was crossing the threshold of his longings, burning through his flesh like a torch. This revelation had nothing to do with Ethel, but with Fabian and Maryana. The fog in his memory was clearing. Maryana had been in love with Fabian. Fabian was in love with Maryana, too.

Why didn't Fabian propose to Maryana? Did he know? Was Maryana's passion always guarded and concealed? Did Fabian ever let his love known to Maryana? Why did he marry?

Dreams and visions were following at Gable's heels. Ethel was with him inside the vacuum of his own betrayal. And yet, she was the queen of his delirium, reigning beyond reason, spinning the web of destiny. She was awesome and awful, brandishing accusations, laughing and mocking.

What if Fabian drops dead?The dry, uncurling wand of lightning had struck Gable's soul. His whole body felt numb and shivering as if the winter blasts had invaded the cell of his solitude and solitary contemplations. His pacing was dwindling to plodding; the lumpish weakness in his legs now heavy. Some sort of stupor, lit by the absurdity of fire and ice was enveloping his body and mind. His feet were guiding him out of his room, down the staircase, and into the parlor where Davie sat at the piano contemplating the black and ivory keys in utter silence.

"Decisions most mundane and difficult," was Gable's thoughtless comment directed at Davie's back. "If you are not sure what to play, may I request Beethoven's Fifth Symphony?" He trooped past him and then stood gazing.

"A strange request as compared to what you always want me to play, Mozart. Chopin would suit your mood, I guess, for pain and madness is oozing out of each pore of your body." He smiled. "But why Beethoven? I don't seem to catch the drift of your mood."

"My mood has nothing to do with my choice. I have heard you play Beethoven, your fingers worship the very notes they touch, and the affect is soothing."

"No matter how soothing, Gable, it won't appease your soul," Davie said. "Neither books, nor music; nothing would offer you peace. Writing, perhaps, if you try. What were you doing in your room, kicking the demons out of your very heels?"

"What in the name of absurdity made you say that?"

"Because you were pounding the floor with your pacing, and I was afraid that the ceiling would crash right over my head." Davie groped for wit and gaiety, but failed. "If you find no outlet for your pain, it would fester inside you and grow cankerous. No use pretending that you are the happiest of men on earth?"

"Who is?" Gable sank into a chair nearby. "Only fools and saints claim to possess this so-called happiness. Isn't it just a word, illusive, formless, and nonexistent? And yet we all strive for it? Little whiffs of joy and peace we might experience now and then, but the interludes make us long for something which is not there. Could that be happiness, our worthy tormentor. Pain festers, Davie, but scars heal.

That's how I feel? There is no pain, yet this senseless ache, some sort of mute longing to be near Ethel, I do admit."

"Ethel deceived you, you must acknowledge that." Davie unsheathed the dagger of reason to dig deep into the heart of reality. "You need to forgive and forget her, not entertaining any hopes of nearness, as you put it. This thought of *nearness* alone is your foe, Gable. It could lead you to follies. You must kill it before it turns into the demon of need and desire," he added hopelessly.

"In my thoughts, Davie, there are no demons but angels. In my thoughts, she is not the deceiver but deceived," Gable declared poetically. "In my thoughts, she is my one and only beloved."

"That's what I fear, Gable, your thoughts." Davie looked into his eyes, trying his best to evoke the sense of reality. "In your thoughts alone, you cannot live. Would you suffer to live, loving her in your thoughts alone?"

"Hope, you never fall in love, Davie," Gable commented. His thoughts were in a stalemate, fleeing pell-mell at the sudden appearance of Aslam.

"Don't mind my intrusion. Keep the fires of your discussion raging." Aslam bristled with good humor, noticing the silence of the brothers.

"How priggish as ever. What a pleasant surprise." Gable leaped to his feet, shaking his friend's hand with a burst of delight.

"Your mom, gracious as ever, granted me the liberty to prowl, or you would have had no pleasant surprise." Aslam laughed, tossing a greeting at Davie.

"It wouldn't surprise me if you came floating down from the very roof top," Gable quipped. "What surprises me is that you have turned off the greed-machine of your medical profession to visit a friend."

"Greed-machine is still on, my friend, I told my patients to take a nap. They'll be charged for this luxury, too." Aslam's eyes twinkled with mischief.

"Such heavy bantering would exhaust you both. May I suggest that you make yourselves comfortable?" Davie indicated the chairs with a quick wave of his arms.

"Yes, my Master." Gable dipped his head in one flourish of a curtsy. "We must sit down. Davie would delight us with a heavenly piece of music." He offered Aslam a chair, abandoning himself on his former seat. "What would you request Davie to play?"

"Mozart." Aslam beamed.

"What a handsome trio you make," Mrs. Faulkner exclaimed as she came upon them unnoticed. "Have to go to that chocolate extravaganza, a sort of fund-raiser." She smiled, sweeping her gaze over all three hurriedly. "Caroline has set lunch on the table, she will make you fresh coffee. Got to go."

"I was hungry, Mom, so I ate early. No need to bother Caroline about that." Davie said goodbye.

"Oh, my poor baby." Mrs. Faulkner turned back. "Forgot to tell Caroline to fix you a hot cup of soup, you don't like cold sandwiches."

"Ham sandwich, it was delicious, Mom." Davie smiled sweetly. "Caroline fixed me hot chocolate, didn't she tell you?"

"Look, who is the pampered one around here?" Gable shot this comment at Aslam, mischief alighting in his eyes as he shifted his gaze toward his mother.

"A cold feast is waiting for you and your friend in the dining room, you better grab it before it turns stale." Mrs. Faulkner caught and held Gable's mischief into her own laughing eyes. "Leave Davie alone, he has audition this evening and he must practice." She flitted out of the room after bestowing a kind smile at Aslam.

"At least some of us have the hope and the luxury to look forward to a bright future." Gable stood and continued, "Come, Aslam, let's leave this genius to his own world of fortunes." He dragged his friend along with him.

"Didn't your mom say, don't tease him?" Aslam protested.

"She only said, leave him alone." Gable bounced out of the room, Aslam following him.

Davie's mirth, not music followed them at their heels. They sat in the large dining room, warmed by the flood of sunshine. The ornate china cabinet laden with crystal was radiating its own glory and warmth as the two friends sat talking and eating.

"So, old and faithful Caroline is still with you?" Aslam commented after being sated with cold sandwiches and blueberry muffins.

"The only few faithful who have no place to go," Gable responded with stoic reserve, eliciting a cheerful expression. "You didn't invite me to your wedding, but accept my heartfelt congratulations," he added. "I was hoping you'd marry some jewel of the east, but you ended up marrying a plain, American girl. She is pretty, though, I hear."

"As compared to the golden goddess' of America, the houris of the east lose their charm," Aslam quipped. "The goddess' of gold and ivory are all here. Yet my wife Heather was born in London, but her parents migrated and settled here."

"You must be dreaming, white is dull, and no amount of tanning lends them the smoothness of gold. And ivory, only Greek goddess' could boast of such complexion," Gable demurred aloud.

"Ah, the blue-eyed goddess' with gold shining on their heads," Aslam declared happily. "Isn't it ironic that the girls in Pakistan who are olive-skinned go through endless pains to make themselves look fair, while the white girls here spend fortunes to look tanned? But you don't find the white girls unattractive, do you?"

"Mostly, yes, with a few exceptions, of course." Gable responded with a broad grin. "Your wife, Heather, granted she is witty and charming, but she is no goddess, I assure you. Unless, of course, you deem her to be so."

"I worship the ground she walks on, if that qualifies her as a goddess?" Aslam laughed. "How is the world treating you after your act of euthanasia?" he asked.

"As the world treats all convicts, with contempt polished by arrogance," Gable declared. "Wonder, how one can measure any act as being noble or wicked? Can one truly judge actions, or draw lines where evil begins or where virtue ends? My editor friend at the local newspaper told me that he couldn't afford to hire an ex-convict. Dad's friend barely managed to find me a job in the small publishing house. My colleagues over there shun me as the plague, except for Bryan. He is too stupid and good-hearted, and his open contempt is rather refreshing, mainly directed at my critiques. Well, that is the world, cold and friendless as ever." He concluded, "I thought I had friends?"

"Didn't know you were that naïve? The word *friend* itself is an imprecation, and with no friendly connotation either," Aslam said. "No one can boast of friends, but acquaintances, dubbed as friends. Selfish parasites as we are we can't help but feed ourselves on our instincts base and gluttonous. Friendship is just a cloak we all must wear to hide our passions of greed and deceit, isn't that obvious?" He chuckled hysterically.

"You sound as if you personally have been deceived by some friends called parasites," Gable said.

"If I were deceived I would probably offer my deepest gratitude — sympathies, perhaps," Aslam sang more than commented. "The truth is that a few whom I deemed friends betrayed my trust by the very virtue of their cold indifference. After learning about the death of my father, they rather pretended ignorance than to offer condolences."

"Am I one of those? Sorry, I didn't know. But my heartfelt condolences, though words fail me on such occasions." Gable showed a genuine concern.

"If you were one of them, I would have never forgiven you since you are not dubbed as an acquaintance," Aslam chortled. "Besides, the ones who sort of teased my raw wounds belong to the class of bigots and hypocrites, their hearts as cold as ice, and their looks glazed with the zeal of piety, my own Muslim brethren. So heartwarming it was to receive cards and flowers from the friends of diverse faiths; especially, when utter neglect from the faithful of my own faith had pierced my heart with pincers of anguish. Only to realize that they were friends of no one, but enemies to their own souls, corrupted with the waters of false piety and self-righteousness. Wealthy and educated they are, yet blind and ignorant to moral obligations."

"Wealth and education fails to tame the brutes in us," Gable declared. "Were you not upset when your sister married someone below her status, in your estimation?" He began evasively, overwhelmed by this abrupt assault of bitterness against Fabian. "You wanted her to marry a doctor, and her choice fell on a clerk, if I am not mistaken. Hope, she has no regrets."

"No regrets, I am sure, but she is unhappy. That much I know." Aslam averted his gaze to the floral arrangement on the mantel. "She told me jokingly not too long ago that she hates to work. And said, 'The saddest thing in this world is this, Aslam, when a husband says: honey, both of us have to work to meet our expenses.' She thinks that her husband's earnings are enough for a comfortable living, but his tastes are extravagant. Dreaming about a bigger house, expensive cars, and luxurious resorts for vacations. When both work, petty arguments surface. Who is going to cook? Who is going to do the laundry? I don't understand. It's not like back-home, even when a wife chooses to work, servants share the burden of the household. And any middle-class family can afford servants. It's different here when the wife ends up working, at home and outside home."

"Needs, if not worries have created this style of living. The disadvantages of status and commercialism in New Age America. Traditional families are thinning out and yuppies taking charge of the godless America," Gable expounded, his heart courting restlessness.

"This world of cellophane prides and prejudices is not to my taste." Aslam, too, was losing interest in this topic.

"Is Heather working?" Gable prodded with a dint of amusement.

"She has not only stopped working outside home, but at home, too." Aslam laughed. "We have a live-in maid, and Heather has the luxury to read or write. She writes poetry and is trying her hand at stories. I'm still smarting against her confession, honest as it may seem, that she loves my status and wealth as much as me." He paused, his look enigmatic. "You will be going to Fabian's this evening, won't you?"

"Yes." Gable elicited a bright smile.

"Your stoicism frightens me, to tell you the truth," Aslam began with a sudden vehemence. "You are custom-made for suffering. You will never forget Ethel. Maybe become a victim of dissipation. Hoping, always, to win her back. Take my advice, look deep within you, and try to heal your wounds. Forget Ethel."

"How well you know me? Sorry, can't take your advice," Gable replied.

"I was afraid of that." Aslam got to his feet. "Should be going. Heather must be waiting, thinking that I'm still at the office."

"Could offer you ham sandwich as a bribe, but you don't eat ham." Gable teased capriciously. "Caroline will fix you a steak if you promise to stay, her specialty, you know." Gable coaxed rather fervently.

"How sensitive you are, my Machiavellian friend." Aslam laughed. "At your table, if you had a Jew, Jain, Hindu and a Muslim as your guests, you would have whale of a time pleasing everyone." He shook hands with him and marched away.

"Goodbye." Gable stood there motionless, alone and forlorn.

Five ~ Laughing Linda

The Sun was dipping west as Gable reached Fabian's home, the party in full swing in their back yard. He was discomforted by his natty appearance, loathing the very neatness of his white shirt, black trousers and polished shoes. The blue in his eyes was like ice against his pale features. His hair was ruffled by the breeze, its silken gold spilling over his brow. The scent of roses was in the air, teasing his senses, as he landed straight into the arena of gaiety where even the lawn chairs were gilded in ochre and vermilion from the dusk.

"Hello, Gable." Fabian held out his hand. "Late as usual. Can't recall a single instance when you treated time with respect."

"Didn't disappoint you then," Gable retorted. "It is very difficult to discipline oneself in the virtues of sloth and banality?"

"I am in no mood to disagree with you. Besides, all the slothful and besotted friends are longing to have the pleasure of your company," Fabian quipped. "I'm not sure if I am thrilled to have you back, but who cares?" He laughed.

"Feel honored to be admitted into this patrician circle of friends," Gable exclaimed, unable to conceal his sarcasm or bitterness. He was about to add more when Ethel came sailing toward them like an angel from the heavens.

"Hello, Gable." Ethel forced her hand into his, the blue in her eyes sparkling.

"You look so pretty in blue, the color of your eyes, exactly," Gable said admiringly.

"Thank you, Gable, gallant as ever." Ethel snatched her hand away, her attention diverted to Tom who was making his presence known.

"Hi, old chap." Tom swaggered toward Gable, boisterous and inebriated. "What happened to your Roman physique, you have lost a lot of weight?" He chuckled.

"Weight is the only thing all of us are grateful to lose," Gable replied. "Predictable as ever, you are grandly drunk. A few more drinks and you'd be sober as a monk."

"Here comes, Linda, the nymph of the paradise," Fabian announced while hugging Ethel.

"Hi, handsome." Linda greeted Gable, ignoring the rest. "Thought, you had abandoned us. Imagine, deserting your friends when they needed you the most, and we did, believe me."

"Had no intention of deserting my friends, most of all, you," Gable responded. "I was yanked out of my cell by the power of your beautiful eyes alone," he added.

"A great compliment, Gable, if you only knew?" Linda was, half drunk, half exultant.

"I could use some crumbs of compliments. Throw some at me, Gable." Fabian tugged at Gable's arm. "We are not going to stand here all evening, are we?" He dragged him along, beckoning the *dears* and the *drunks* to follow.

The evening had dwindled into a balmy night. Gable seemed to be lost into the pools of levity and ideation thrown open before him by his friends. The most garrulous amongst them were Aaron and Linden, pressed by their own needs to dive into the ocean of absurdities. All seemed happy, beer and liquor coursing in their veins, and their faces flushed with excitement. Gable was cherishing his fifth glass of rum and Coke while hotdogs and hamburgers were sizzling on the grill and conversations rising to the height of absurdity. Ethel was fluttering around acting as perfect hostess, inviting all to enjoy the fruits and the salads, all displayed neatly on one long table by the barbecue grille. Fabian was nowhere in sight, and to Gable's dreamy awareness, the lights on the lampposts looked dull and foggy. Suddenly, he was aware that he was seated opposite Aslam and Heather who were laughing heedlessly and trying to catch his attention.

"Have I been sitting here like a fool, not even knowing that the happiest of couples have honored me with their presence?" Gable was holding both Aslam and Heather prisoner in his smiling gaze. "I hear you are basking in the sunshine of indolence these days?" He teased Heather, stealing a mischievous look at Aslam.

"Aslam," Heather exclaimed while pinching her husband's arm mercilessly.

"Ouch," Aslam screamed. "I'm not protesting, though pain is intolerable." He braced himself for defense. "Don't believe him, love, he is a potful of lies. You'll get to know him soon, and then you won't believe a word he says. Didn't he wish us happiness? Look at him now. Do you think he believes in happiness?" He shot a challenging look at Gable.

"That's why I can never attain it," Gable said thoughtlessly.

"You have lost it—" Aslam bit his tongue, his look apologetic.

"Aslam," chided Heather. "Doom and gloom are not allowed here this evening." She sprang to her feet.

"Yes. I'm starving." Aslam sprinted to his feet, inviting Gable toward the table.

"You got here late, too?" Gable demurred aloud, coasting along with the happy couple. "Perfect timing though, rounds of bear almost done and stomachs churning for food."

"Couldn't get away. Told my patients to take a nap, but they wouldn't listen," Aslam responded. "Pleaded with Heather to go on her own, *don't wait for me,* but she wouldn't listen either."

"I can't eat when he's not around," Heather explained laughingly. "My secret to staying slim, because he is never around." She picked up a stack of plastic plates, offering all, including Gable and her husband.

"My heart is open to this vice of pleasure and gluttony." Aslam claimed his plate, noticing Ethel hovering close at the end of the table.

"Vice aside, Aslam, you don't deserve the pleasure of gluttony. How atrocious of you to come so late." Ethel shot him a reproof.

Aslam began to laugh, Heather pounding him with her own gentle blows, while Gable stood there gazing at Ethel. The familiar ache of love was tearing the fabric of his loneliness. Ethel could feel the surge of his mute pain and suffering, and her own heart went fluttering to him.

"Would you like a drink, Gable?" Ethel asked, color rising to her cheeks.

"No." One involuntary sob was torn out of Gable's heart "I mean, yes, I could use some whiskey and soda." He was blinded by the onslaught of his despair.

The early hours of evening on the brink of night were flowing smoothly in rivulets of gaiety. Gable, wading through the flood of his hopelessness, had emerged on the shores of surface-calm. After accepting drink from Ethel, he had immersed himself headlong into the muddied waters of discussions with his friends, wearing a mask of gaiety. Taking the advice of Aslam, he himself had become a glutton, more by drowning himself in alcohol than feasting on meat and salads. Paradoxically, his thoughts were nibbling on feasts sprinkled with the condiments of wounds and longings. Ethel was his *Beloved Incarnate*, his gaze following her in the manner of a suppliant, brimming with love and devotion. The Beloved had settled down near Fabian, arrested in his heart like the portrait of bliss. Aslam and Heather were there, too, and a group of other friends, but Gable's senses were courting oblivion. His thoughts were filled with warning that he was painfully and deliciously drunk, but he was not heeding this warning, only snatching snippets of conversations with a sense of elation. He couldn't connect faces with the voices, but was intoxicated by the sheer novelty of uproar and arguments.

"God? Does God ever leave His Throne to visit us lowly ones on earth and witness our pain and suffering? Is child-abuse sanctioned by the Lord of the Heavens? What right have parents to beat their children mercilessly and demanding respect as their reward for torture and bullying? Where is the reason in this? Where is the sanity, the justification?"

"Your father whipped you when you were a child, who knows? Maybe, he was justified in disciplining a rambunctious child? Wild and untamed specimens of nature's own imperfections as most children are. The children of God. Are parents not endowed with the sense of duty and righteousness, guiding their issues to the right path, and teaching them the values of honesty, discipline, kindness?"

"Since birth, our very souls have been corrupted by the will of God. First, tainting our souls and then punishing us with the fear of doom and gloom. Who could do that to our souls—God, isn't it obvious?"

"Our own selfishness and ingratitude toward life, in life, forces open the doors of doom and gloom, not sanctioned by God. We are to contemplate without heaping blame on God or anyone."

"What choices one has in terms of birth or death? Did anyone ask me if I wanted to be born? Am I not bound by the law of some divine oracle to live the life as ordained? Am I compelled to feel gratitude, too? For what? For this rude, wretched handiwork of God, called life?"

"Would you prefer death over life then?"

"No, I want to live. To live and suffer, forever and forever."

"You have no right to live."

"What gives you the right to be my life's executioner?"

"Your life itself. And you have branded it with the judgment of your own. If you find life dull and worthless, do you deserve to live, ask yourself that."

Gable's thoughts were shutting off all sounds, arrested into their own prison-reflections of the world so wonderful and so very ridiculous. His gaze was returning much too often at the altar of his beloved Ethel, paying homage with mute reverence. Some sort of pain and elation had settled within his thoughts, flashing him glimpses of life, jewel-bright and pain-filled. Ruby-red was the color of mortality. Primal sins had the glow of ivory. The wounds inside the hearts were gold, and lusts were colored with the rude brushstroke of vermilion. Ochre torments and reveries saffron were mists illusive and frolicking. He himself was caught inside the unreality of ether, exploring the chasms boundless, and breathing eternally the scent of time and timelessness. So immersed was he inside the unreality of his own quiet journeys, depicting the valleys of non-birth and non-existence, that he was startled by the voice of Fabian, urging all to a game of Russian rummy.

"We haven't played cards for weeks. I plan to retrieve all that I have spent on this barbecue, so get your wallets out and let the bets rolling," Fabian proclaimed.

The tables were joined together and the chairs pulled closer, creating an island to place bets and shout wagers. Shouting and excitement were familiar to Gable, his head spinning under the weight of inebriation. The girls were cheating as usual, heaping their rewards in front of them with unashamed hilarity. Linden was bluffing, ignoring the trail of his losses, and hoping for a streak of luck. Ethel and Fabian were graciously lending losers the funds from the depleted reserve of the bank. Aslam and Heather were playing recklessly, doubling their bets, and accruing debts which they couldn't pay. Gable was oblivious to his gains or losses. His gaze was still lured to his beloved Ethel, sending spasms of pain down his chest, the pain of betrayal from his beloved.

The evening had dwindled into the bosom of a starry night, and Russian rummy was no closer to lull the players to sleep. Gable was deliciously drunk. He was attracted by the beauty and laughter of Linda, the demon of lust inside him awakening with the primal violence of a need both brutal and savage. His thoughts were dancing around the painted face of Linda, seized by a terrible impulse to blind her wild, lovely eyes, to disfigure her lips with kisses, and to consume her entirely.

"I have wasted half this night playing this absurd game and this is my reward?" Linden was counting his losses.

"My reward is that I have ended up even," someone at the far end of the table said dejectedly.

"My last two lucky dollars and my wallet is empty," Tom grumbled.

"I am paying for my own dinner and in my own house, too, and you better cherish this money." Fabian was reluctant to part with his five-dollar bill, as Aaron snatched it away from his hand.

Gable staggered to his feet, his gaze devouring Linda seated opposite. Amidst the flurry of laughter and arguments, no one even noticed that Gable was sauntering away, except for Linda, who was following him as if hypnotized. Gable's feet came to a standstill, his gaze shooting up to the sky, the moon arrested in a canopy of stars filling his drunken thoughts with awe. Linda crept closer, her own eyes fixed to the cold, stabbing stars with intensity akin to envy. Both were silent, suspended in their own world, the essence of time lost to them, not even noticing that friends were floating this way in eddies of farewell to reach their cars. An imperceptible shudder shook Gable's sturdy frame as he turned abruptly facing Linda, the brilliance of stars reflected in his eyes.

"How beautiful you are," Gable whispered, gazing into her eyes. "Would you have dinner with me Friday night?"

"Yes." Noticing the approach of Aslam and Heather, she fled.

"I couldn't help but hear, Gable. You are writing your own fate by inviting her to dinner—an unwise decision," Aslam warned, his cigarette poised before him as he blew out rings of smoke.

"Would you erase it and rewrite it to suit the precepts of wisdom?" Gable's look was thoughtful and piercing.

"A portion of it must be deleted if I'm permitted the risk of erasing?" Aslam puffed on his cigarette belligerently.

"What would you ...." Gable could not continue, espying the leisurely approach of Ethel and Fabian.

"You will be forbidden to see Ethel, the first commandment." Aslam said quietly, noticing the adorable couple coming closer.

"This commandment is tainted with the reek of disobedience," Gable quipped hopelessly. "May I have a cigarette?"

"Doctors don't recommend smoking?" Aslam was quick to offer him one.

"A gift from the bounties of God." Gable let Aslam hold the light for him while he puffed on it voraciously.

"I could have never guessed in a million years that you smoked

"Leave it to Aslam. He tempts all to smoke to earn his daily bread." Heather broke her silence, laughter trilling down her lips.

"Your guess is good as mine." Gable smiled, stealing a look at Ethel, his heart thundering with the violence of a hurricane. "The gifts of Providence, how dare we shun?" His thoughts were longing. "Goodbye, something tells me that I must not say another word." He cantered away as if fleeing the very angels of the heavens and demons of the earth.

Six ~ First Date

Gable was pacing in his room, indulging in this ritual of his sanity and contemplation. An entire week of frenzy and delirium since the party at Fabian had flitted past, and Gable was nowhere near the shores of reconciliation with his inner torment and outward calm. He had just returned from work, awakening to the vague sense of reality that it was Friday and he had no friends with whom he could invade the bars, or drown the loathsome hours of the evening in dull discussions. While pacing, he was jolted to awareness by another stab of a reality, that he had a dinner date with Linda. All week Linda had been banished from his thoughts, his head tortured by torments indescribable, Ethel reigning over each cell of insanity in his very being.

Now that Linda had popped up in Gable's head like a thorn brittle, his pacing was getting as wild as his thoughts. Ethel was still with him, a *lovely rose*, wafting forth the scent of healing, yet the agonies of his soul were not appeased. His thoughts were feverish and cankerous, spitting out bitterness. The demons of his longings were let loose, his tortured spirit captive.

Why do you need to see Linda? Gable's thoughts were commencing a rude interrogation. *You can't live without Ethel. How would you suffer the agony of banishing her from your thoughts? How long would you survive, living only with the scent of her presence? Will you ever?* His thoughts were snipped loose by the loud urgency in Davie's voice.

"Gable. Stop pounding the floor and get the phone. Bryan is on the line."

"Be right there." Gable murmured dashing down the stairs.

Davie held out the phone, which he claimed eagerly, eliciting a thin smile. Davie wheeled back to his own chamber of music. Gable leaned against the wall to collect his thoughts.

"Don't you have anything better to do on a Friday evening than to call a hated colleague of yours?" Gable said with a false sense of euphoria.

"My evening is nothing short of lust and libido, but duty compels me to humor my witless friend. Some sort of philanthropic curse or impulse, you might say," Bryan chortled in a sing-song refrain.

"A miracle, even to expect any sense of guilt from you," Gable quipped, making his voice as cheerful as possible. "I am all ears, go ahead, shoot."

"You have your hands on the most coveted of assignments." Bryan's voice was charged with the currents of excitement. "You are to interview that reprobate, good-for-nothing veteran, whose scandalous past can't wait to explode."

"You mean, William Bailey?" Gable tonelessly inquired.

"Your enthusiasm is killing me." Bryan breathed disdain. "If you don't like this assignment, I would be delighted to relieve you off this burden. So much fun to yank the ladder of fame to success from right under your feet. You have the talent to write that kind of stuff, I loathe to admit, mind you."

"How can you judge my excitement, or the lack of it, on the phone? If you were here, you would see me jumping up and down." A sad smile was creasing the ridges around Gable's lips as he continued, "Save your flatteries though, and do not underestimate the heat of my curiosity. Is this the same stag whose ego is as big as a mountain and his pride as high as the highest peaks of the Himalayas?"

"The very same. That proud frump. Priggish and vainglorious." Bryan was garnishing his epithets with a snort of mirth. "His better-half, or worst baggage, just landed in our little town of Springfield. He is quite stunned, I hear."

"That worst baggage as you call it, must contain the virtue of beauty, if nothing else?" Gable commented with a stab at enthusiasm.

"You are so dry and witless, Gable, and you are not listening," Bryan chided. "William had married some whore in Singapore, concealing the whole affair from his American wife. For how many years, God knows? He came back a few months ago, and now this wife with two teenagers shows up. It seems she didn't know he was married. She is more furious than shocked, demanding fortunes, if not explanations? Oh, what a scandal, what a scandal."

"I can't imagine him groveling before his lawfully wedded wife in America, or acknowledging the demands of the one so wickedly wronged in Singapore." Gable pumped a little animation into his voice.

"Unpleasant shock for both, I'm sure." Bryan's excitement was deflated. "I must go and seek my flower-girl, whoever she may be? Goodbye." He hung up the phone abruptly.

Gable replaced the phone in the cradle on the wall, standing inert and brooding. His thoughts were a whirlwind. They were spinning some absurd links between words and actions, witnessing the mangled corpses of hopes deformed. And yet there was fresh odor of life in chaos and deformity, something liquid and wholesome oozing out of the pores of hopelessness. His thoughts were kindling the flames of delusions, and aiming for the flint of reality.

How wretched is man, how small and insignificant, clutching at the reeds of hopes, yet sinking deeper and deeper into the vortex of despair? Gable's thoughts were tugging at his awareness to stir him to action. *Linda would be furious, sitting in the restaurant all by herself, feeling forsaken, neglected.* He was racing toward the door as if whipped by the demons of guilt and torment.

Buzzing through the freeway with no thought of speed limit, Gable was in a haste to reach the Chinese restaurant where he was supposed to join Linda for dinner. His thoughts were light and feverish, shooting up as if filled with helium, and swooping down as if hit by the fury of the meteors. The restaurant was only a few miles from his home and he had reached there without attracting any policemen. But his head was throbbing, as if he had suffered a major crash.

You are writing your own fate. Gable's thoughts were echoing this epigram of Aslam with ferocity akin to murder.

Yes, I might propose to Linda. Get married. Fulfill the prophecy of Aslam. Truly, write my own fate. Getting married? A desecration at the altar of love within me. Breeding children out of a loveless marriage, suffering and pretending to be happy. Isn't this the way all the married couples live, happy forever, suffering eternally? He was whisked straight into the world of torment and reality.

"Sorry, I am late, Linda, could you forgive me?" Gable pulled up a chair opposite her, and fell into it as if crestfallen. "I was about to leave when one of my colleagues called. His name is Bryan, he talked endlessly, and all he wanted to tell me was that he had an important assignment lined up for me. Well, that's unimportant. I wanted to be with you, and here I am, late, trying to find right words to apologize."

"You have, Gable, and I understand. No need to apologize, really

"Would you like to order a drink before dinner?" A waitress materialized before Gable could respond.

"Whiskey and soda, please." Gable breathed exigently, watching the waitress disappear. "You have not forgiven me, really?" He returned his attention to Linda who seemed rather sullen.

"Sitting here all alone for the past twenty minutes is no fun." Linda laughed suddenly, her lips pouting under the weight of accusations. "Only a bottle of wine to keep me company while I pretended that I am perfectly content."

A veil of silence was drawn over them as the waitress procured Gable's drink, smiling graciously and asking if they were ready to order dinner. The silence was broken as both placed their orders, but a banquet of constraint was spread between them. Gable could feel the sting of chill and silence, his thoughts themselves one lump of ice and awkwardness.

"I do not blame you for not forgiving me. I deserve it," Gable said, draining away half of his drink in one large gulp.

"It's not the first time that my date showed up late." Linda laughed.

"Yes, all those dolts, and I am no different than any of them," Gable quipped deliriously. "With the exception that I am in love." He could feel the blood rushing to his cheeks, as if white lies in his head were painting his cheeks red.

"You don't expect me to believe in this—do you? Sorry, it's just that I have heard this word *love* so often that it has lost its meaning for me." She almost choked on her wine.

"You break my heart, Linda. You think I am just saying that?" Gable assumed an expression both sincere and woebegone.

"This expression in your eyes, Gable, it doesn't suit you. A classic one though, of men who think they've been wronged most heartlessly. Are you thinking about Ethel?"

"Ethel. Who?" Gable contrived a smile.

"Next time, you'll be saying, Linda, who? To your other friends." Linda contrived a smile.

"I'm a fool, but not that fickle." Gable breathed contritely. "To tell you the truth, I have neither forgotten Ethel, nor forgiven her. Trying to forget her, if you are kind enough to believe this. This evening, I will never forget even if I tried. Your beautiful eyes will haunt me forever."

"When I am past getting used to your flatteries, I might even begin to believe you," Linda chirped hilariously. "Right now, just my vanity is tickled."

"Your eyes *are* beautiful, dear Linda, and that's no flattery. Friends forever." He raised his glass.

"Maybe." Linda's eyes were gathering a mist of tears as she could not stop laughing.

Seven ~ Children of God

Gable was seated at his desk in his room, blackening page after page in some feverish haste, not even knowing what he was writing. He had been sitting there for hours, oblivious to time and surroundings. His parents had left early for Columbus to spend this Saturday with their friends. Davie had been out on his tour of recitals for the entire weekend, and Gable had found time to start his novel which had been throbbing inside his head like a wound. *Children of God*, he had repeated this title over and over again in his head before it could appear on the paper, sloughing off its holy mask, and spilling the abscess in his thoughts which could not claim even a trace of sanctity.

Gable's room was an unholy clutter, an ashtray brimming with cigarette stubs and a bottle of whiskey half empty. His thoughts were drained of all vigor, but he was dragging them along on the piece of paper with a will most brutal and savage. Caroline had left some sandwiches for him in the dining-room, and he had nibbled on them absently before returning to his prison of clutter. This prison was now reeking of alcohol and tobacco, but he seemed oblivious to the foul odor as he kept smoking and scribbling. He didn't care what he wrote, or if he would be able to read later what he had written, only aware that the act of writing itself was therapeutic, bandaging the wounds in his soul with the promise of healing.

Is my soul healed? Gable thought suddenly, the pen poised before him like a dagger. *Three bleating months of misery and torment, all scattered, all returning.* One bubble of a recollection was snapping lose in his head, followed by loud mirth from the painted lips of Linda. *How can I ever erase the memory of Ethel? Can't forget the Unforgettable. Author of my own fate, am I? Where lies the salvation? In marriage. Is that going to be my Cross and Crucifixion? At least I am not in love with Linda, so there is no danger of hating her. Would she marry me? She has not said, yes.*

Gable's thoughts sent a certainty that she would marry him. Why, he didn't know? The pen was slipping through his fingers, his other hand reaching for a cigarette. Since his first date with Linda, he had a feeling that she was attracted toward him, but what he didn't know was that she had fallen in love with him, utterly and besottedly had fallen in love with him. Had he known that, he'd have never seen her again, but as it was, he was blissfully and wretchedly ignorant. Davie was more perceptive. After seeing this odd couple as his brother and girl-friend, he had warned Gable with a subtle hint of tragedy in the future.

Do not even think of getting married to Linda. You would regret it, would make her utterly unhappy. You should not ever marry — anyone. Davie's warning was now hitting Gable's head with sparks of fire which had nothing to do with Davie.

You are not fated to remain celibate, Gable, but you would suffer. Suffer terribly, if you married Linda. We all plunge into this baptismal fountain of matrimony, hoping to be cleansed, but ending up utterly disappointed. Aslam's sanctimonious comments were pounding Gable's head, but he was becoming aware of the door-bell.

Abandoning the cigarette in his glass of whiskey, he raced down the steps, throwing open the front doors in a state of agitation. Fabian stood there smiling, his hand held out and mischief shining in his eyes.

"You are all alone?" Gable muttered disappointment, peering out to see if Ethel was lurking out there somewhere.

"Yes. And I'm in amorous mood, too." Fabian offered his cheek all the while laughing. "Is it a requirement to bring an army of guards while visiting a friend?" He continued mischievously, "Yes, I came all by myself. Ethel doesn't want to see you. She is upset that you have forgotten us and says don't bother to visit us? Well, to be honest, she has gone to a bridge party. How dark it is in here. A Pluto in Hades. Aren't you going to invite me in?"

"Welcome to the darkness of the Hades. Won't you come in?" Gable said.

"I am in no mood to face Persephone this gloomy evening." Fabian laughed again. "Let's go out. Have you eaten?"

"Not really hungry."

"Who cares? I'm starving. We will find some sordid, little place to talk and dine. I am in a mood to splurge, dollars bursting out of my pockets." Fabian's good humor was not willing to accept any excuses.

"Some sleazy bar, I reckon?" The twig of dry wit in Gable's head was crackling. "You are not dressed properly to go near the sanctuary of that Underworld."

"You are not dressed for a ball, either?" Fabian dived deep into the pool of his friend's mirth, dragging him out on the porch.

The gloom and darkness of the evening could not be seen inside the Marble Flake Bar & Grille, which Gable and Fabian had chosen to dine, and to resurrect the memories of old friendship and days of carefree abandon. They seemed oblivious to the odor of sweat and grease, attacking their fried chicken as if famished for months. The music was loud, and the windowless room filled with smoke, while the bartender kept filling their beer glasses. Fabian was scooping the remnants of his mashed potatoes into his fork and feeling a sense of euphoria, his look brimming with animation.

"Can't imagine, you and Linda dating for three whole months and neglecting your good friends altogether." Fabian was trying to drown the din of other voices by pumping his own lungs to full blast.

"You have the cheek to complain, my friend?" Gable's own response was loud and gleeful. "Who has neglected who, is debatable. My colleagues at work drop in often, Aslam and Heather have come to see me. I haven't had time, I admit, but I have gone to see Maryana." His voice was suddenly choked. "You two never even thought of visiting me, you must admit."

"Don't blame me. Your own damned pride, if you only knew," Fabian retorted evasively.

"Linda and I are getting married."

"Gable." Fabian looked glazed.

"Don't look so appalled, Fabian. I'm not about to commit an act of sin or violence, am I?" Gable was deliciously drunk with the draughts of his own pain.

"A loveless marriage? Worse than any sin or crime," Fabian replied.

"Who knows? I have proposed, but I haven't received the sinful *yes* yet?"

"No doubt, she will say, yes." Fabian contrived a pale smile. "Fates can neither be altered nor averted, as the Greeks say," he added, with a stab at derision.

"Just curiosity, how did you know I was dating Linda; considering, that we didn't see each other for three whole months?"

"Small world, isn't it?" Fabian intoned evasively.

"Smaller than a woman's heart, I predict." Gable could taste the warmth and sweetness of beer in his very thoughts. "Those ineffable secrets which flower inside a woman's heart. But then they turn into weeds, wild and multiplying, and choking by their own *need* to spill their seeds into the *heart* of the world, all-knowing. That's where secrets breed and gossips sprout. A small world, indeed."

"The sheen of wisdom is drained clear out of your epigrams." Fabian chuckled with a burst of excitement. "It seems so long ago, those witless discussions, and hours of ideation and idleness? Centuries ago, you were in prison, and I was out there somewhere, physically and emotionally drained. And all that time, *time* was playing tricks on me. Things would have been different, if ...." Fabian was confessing his guilt against the veil of his incoherence.

"Time," Gable said heedlessly. *"Eternity itself rests in unity, and this image we call time,"* Gable quoted, lighting up another cigarette.

"Plato, if I am not mistaken?" Fabian breathed avidly.

"Those long hours of witless discussions, Fabian, were hollow inside out, no wisdom, no knowledge. Rather worthless. No need to resurrect them."

"I don't think our discussions were worthless. We got to meet authors mad and strange through their words, if not through their deeds." Fabian was anxious to unroll the carpet of long-lost conversations.

"Senseless all, I insist." Gable was adamant in sticking to his own point of view.

"You disappoint me." Fabian was feeling the rungs of sobriety, where pain and guilt lay trampled.

"In what respect?" Gable puffed on his cigarette.

"In not detesting me as you should?" Fabian spewed out his guilt, dreading the outcome of this conversation.

"How do you know, I don't?" Gable flashed him an enigmatic look. "I don't hate you, you can be rest assured," he added thoughtfully.

"A fat morsel of assurance to swallow." Fabian began recklessly. "Besides dating Linda and wallowing into the puddles of pain and loneliness, what else do you do? For pleasure, I mean. Writing, is that it?" He goaded, as if purging his guilt with the whip of confessions he couldn't voice.

"Have been glued to my desk all day. Tossing pebbles of worthless thoughts, my excursion on the fields of pain and pleasure," Gable admitted, sealing away the cauldron of his own sweet torment.

"Hope, you finish what you started. What is the topic of your inspiration this time?" Fabian was earnest in renewing the link of their former friendship.

"Nothing inspirational, just banalities. Trying to catch a glimpse of the *mystery* in life and death," Gable said.

"You won't find anything interesting in both and nothing mysterious, either. But, what have you discovered so far?" Fabian ordered another jug of beer.

"They are not two, but *one*, if one dares explore the slippery roads of life and death. A river of illusions, this life. Diving deep into the muddied waters of death and then bouncing back to the pulse of life, again and forever. More waves of illusions following a succession of death and rebirth, proclaiming oneness, changelessness." Gable's thoughts were repeating what he had written in a state of feverish delirium.

"Strange and foolish. Might as well wear a dunce's cap and go dancing on the streets, naked?" Fabian teased. "Your intellect has run dry, and your intelligence gone all haywire."

"Fools are blessed with the gold of wit, which I lack, so am not qualified to wear a dunce's cap." Gable was caught into the eddy of his own thoughts. "One *single life* and many deaths in between, still rendering life not lifeless. Do we not die a million deaths when each little stab of pain, loss, or grief cuts through our souls with the naked steel of torture and tyranny? Yet, we die not, living over the mounds of sorrow and hopelessness, and growing strong and resilient. Then death, this bubble of illusion, the womb of life, giving birth and cradling life back into its own womb. A lifetime of imponderables." He made one hopeless gesture, his thoughts shrunk and deflated.

"If that's what you are going to write in your book, then take my advice. Buy a beggar's bowl and go begging for alms, for no one is going to buy your book." Fabian laughed, unable to contain the flood of guilt inside him. "I am making a fool of myself, it's obvious. I'm trying my best to feel at ease, well, to catch that link which made us the best of friends. I know I have hurt you terribly, but I don't know where to begin as to why and how?" His face was flushed, as if ready to explode.

"You're acting like a fool, for sure. And you don't need to whip up any justification." Gable held on to the hem of stoicism. *"No new fashion of hardship, none unexpected rises to confront me; all have I anticipated, all have I traversed in my mind."* He tossed another crumb of quotation, feeling only the whiff nostalgia.

"You and your *Aeneid*, Gable, all that literary jargon you stuffed me with." Fabian attacked with the daggers of his own agitation. "Why don't you admit you're hurting? You're smoking like a chimney. Dating that painted doll of a girl called Linda, why? What in the name of absurdity you are trying to do to yourself? Is your heart your lone tormentor, goading you to ruin yourself? Ask guidance from God, you need it, that's how I feel."

"What in the name of what is what? And whatever that what is, has it anything to do with the world, or God? Something specific to talk about, let's say, *destiny*. Very interesting subject, which liberates us all from any sense of shame, remorse, contrition."

"It's hopeless." Fabian said. "You want to suffer and nothing would appease your suffering. Apologies, justifications, anything, nothing. Writing is your only salvation, I guess. *Catharsis*, you would say. Hold on to it for the sake of your own sanity, then. What were you writing before you, well, I only remember the title? *Philosophy of the Sexes*, wasn't that the one you were working on?"

"What has sex to do with philosophy?" Gable was distorting the meaning of his own chosen title. "Sex is an entity, mute and mindless. Male or female. Mind alone is philosophy and the philosopher. Yet, mind operates independent of the soul, which is perfect, for soul only suffers and mind inspires. Mind is subservient to conscience though, and it obeys this *tyrannous lord*. Conscience. Yes. Gnawing, commanding, and tyrannizing." His vehemence was truncated by this sudden awareness that his thoughts were arrested into a net of absurdities.

"You should not even attempt to write. My own thoughts are chameleon-like, changing without warning?" Fabian seemed to ponder aloud. "You should find comfort in religion, perhaps. Faith brings peace, and salvation."

"*Death by salvation comes gently, gluttony makes me explode.* Ponder upon these words by Seneca, my friend, you might get some answers to your own chameleon-like confusion." Gable's thoughts were wearied.

"When was the last time you went to church or prayed?" Fabian was clinging to some reed of a hope to appease the sufferings of his friend.

"Only bigots and hypocrites go to church," Gable responded.

"Permit me to refresh your memory, Gable." Fabian began with a sudden stab at reality. "You religiously went to church with your parents, even dragged me to a midnight Mass one Christmas Eve?"

"That was when I had not read Nietzsche," Gable admitted reluctantly. "'Jesus starts directly with the condition the, Kingdom of Heaven, in the heart, and he does not find the means to it in the observances of the Jewish church. The reality of Judaism itself he regards as nothing. He is purely inward. Sin, repentance, forgiveness, none of this belongs here, it is acquired from Judaism, or it is pagan.' I have lost faith in God."

"Start reading Aeneid again, Gable. Listen to what your friend Virgil says. "In every man indwells a god, what god we know not."

"Yes, what god," Gable said thoughtfully. "The God of mercy. Or of wrath. The jealous, unforgiving God?" His wearied thoughts were riffling through the pages of the old books. "Must introduce you to the author by the name of J. Krishnamurti. 'The concept of sin, reward, forgiveness, all quite unimportant, and virtually excluded from the primitive practices of Christianity. Now comes the foreground. An appalling mishmash of Judaism and Greek philosophy. Asceticism, continual judging and condemning, order of rank,' etc."

"No use talking about religion to an absolute heathen." Was Fabian's desperate cry of anguish, which had nothing to do with faith, but with guilt. "Just to ease my own conscience, may I unburden my heart as to how and why I got married to Ethel? Hoping, that it would lend you a little comfort, too?" He was appealing, rather requesting.

"Go ahead, shoot. I'm all ears." Gable consented, bracing himself against the deluge of agony and torture.

"Ethel was heartbroken after you went to prison." Fabian began with a grinding haste, lest the shattering truth be left buried forever. "All your friends were, including me. But Ethel and I were thrown together, by chance it seemed, to console each other for the loss, I mean absence, whatever? Don't know how it all began, but we were drawn to each other. Call it love, or affection, am still not sure? The memory of those days is all haze and illusion, some sort of magic and mystery. Whose will we obeyed? Could we condone the fruits of our own actions, or lay the burden of our passions at the feet of some *power*, Supreme and inviolate, I kept thinking." He continued fiercely. "What God indeed, you are right. Us little maggots, naming God the author of our follies. We could very well be the innocent victims? In His court of justice, neither we are the jury, nor the judge. Just some ingrate wretches, voiceless and defenseless. Wearing a noose of guilt. Guilty! All of us, yes, the worms most foul and cankerous, us." He sighed relief, laughing hysterically.

"Victims all, is that the truth?" Gable was sucked into the vortex of his own. "Men and beasts. Or, just *beasts* would qualify us all as lowly victims. What sins we have committed? Whom have we offended? Why must we suffer?"

"The victims of our own ignorance we are. How can we perceive the Unknown and the Invisible?" Fabian's psyche, not mind, was offering this predicament.

"What is there to perceive? Are we not guided by the hands of destiny to stumble and succumb?" Gable began hastily, "Who are we? Where are the gods? Are they sitting up there in the heavens, shooting us with the lightning of laughter, lowering down thundering commands? Which god should be our true lord? Whose commandments ring with the cheers of righteousness? Whose will is nobler than the rest? Piety, faith, holy laws, unholy commandments. Altars strange and tempting. Passions lawful and forbidden. Gods warring and vengeful, raining down tablets carved with contradictions, permitting and forbidding, then sanctioning what has been forbidden, making holy profane, and unholy hallowed." His thoughts were slain by the gleam of mockery in Fabian's eyes.

"Didn't I tell you, Solomon came to me in my dream, saying, 'Belief is lame and faith blind. But both as the crutches to hold on to if one has the strength to persevere. Belief lends sight to faith, and faith offers the staff of life to belief.'"

"God, forgive us our sins." Gable got to his feet.

"Yes, us lowly maggots." Fabian kicked his chair back, fumbling for his wallet in his jean pocket.

Eight ~ Marriage Vows

Gable the bridegroom, dressed in a black tuxedo this memorable evening, was making smoke rings while gazing out of his bedroom window at the dusk. The sky was splashed with puffy clouds, some white, the rest gilded by sunset in hues of saffron and vermilion. His gaze was strange and mysterious, his expression as of a man about to lay his head on the scaffold in hope of meeting his true bride in the afterlife. He wondered if the reward or penalty for this strange rite of unholy matrimony was *death*. Linda, his bride-to-be, was farthest from his thoughts. In fact, he was not thinking at all, only following the memories on the map of time.

One year had slithered past since his release from the prison. The spring of his liberty had bloomed and withered. The summer of his passion, kindling into one small flame, had died into the cold tomb of the winter. He had seen the births and deaths of many seasons within him, each one leaving behind a massacre of hopes and aspirations. Like an actor skillfully trained, he had played the role of a son, a lover, a worker, a brother, but never had he participated in a drama where he was to assume the lead role of a bridegroom. The horror of the stage fright had not yet dawned upon him. His heart was still a blister of pain, loving the torture of love and betrayal and relinquishing not the *memory* of the *unforgettable*.

"Ethel. Beloved." One whisper of tenderness died on Gable's lips, as he stood cloaked in the aura of his oblivion. "My love." Another sweet murmur escaped the silence in his thoughts. "I am getting married."

The sudden assault of this yawning abyss in Gable's thoughts stung him as he stumbled toward the chair at his desk. He flung himself on the hard seat in a sudden fit of despair, the sting of pain licking the soles of his feet as if he had walked on hot coals. With his eyes closed he was trying to catch the glimpse of his bride-to-be, but could only see some faceless vision in the bridal gown. A fever coursed through his veins. Sitting with his head thrown back, he appeared like an actor in the play, the noose of fate tightening around his neck. The hand of death was poised before him, the play had ended and the curtain was closing.

Gable stirred in his seat as if wading through a sea of torment, the stark realization dawning upon him that he was getting married this very evening. He got to his feet swaying, his soul confirming his mad decision in getting married to Linda, reminding him what he had written in his diary, that he was about to sign his own death-warrant. He was pacing, trying to envision the face of his bride out of the muddied waters of his living torment. Instead, the face of Maryana was emerging forth. His heart was cognizant that his sister looked forlorn and unhappy.

The phantoms of our own follies, we. Gable's pace was slackening, his thoughts sharpening the scythe of madness. *The storms rage and the mountains crumble. The raging fury in seasons settles and dissipates, digging deep trenches of devastation, and still the life goes on. The absurdity of it all.* His thoughts were witnessing their own tombstones in words, already buried in paper-graves with the seal of ink. *This grinding wheel of hope and hopelessness, always there somewhere and churning eternally. Tribes and nations die and fade from the books of history, yet one moonlit night studded with stars is enough to whip anyone's heart with longing for one more dawn of life. Bitter, bitter are the sufferings which yawn and explode even in nature, the eclipse and the racing of the stars toward death, what noble powers arrest and*—his thoughts were arrested by the splinter of urgency in his father's voice, commanding him to come down.

The memory of his father's impatience and his warning lest he be late for his own wedding had escaped Gable entirely. In fact, the entire ceremony with Linda as some faceless bride in shimmering lace and pearls were some sort of a phantasmagoric dream. Seated at the garlanded table, drowning a wedge of his wedding cake with wine, Gable seemed to be gazing into the sparkling eyes of his bride as the one possessed. He could see his parents halting at the opposite end of their long table, his mother watching him tenderly.

"That's enough wine for this one evening, Gable," Mrs. Faulkner chided, bestowing a sweet smile at Linda.

"Mother," Gable protested, draining his glass in one quick gulp.

"Our boy is a married man now, Sue, he doesn't need our guidance," Mr. Faulkner chimed in, watching Davie wheel in close to the middle of the center stage.

"You are allowed a few more sips, Gable, for such pleasure is forbidden inside your wedding suite." Davie tossed his own comment brightly. "Mother has posted commandments by your bedside, and one of them forbids drinking." He laughed, joining Linda in her joy.

"Are there any commandments from you which I should follow?" Gable quipped, espying Maryana who was wending her way toward the bridal table.

"I have one commandment for you, Gable, which must be obeyed." Maryana elicited warmth, her pallor stark. "Never lose sight of your bride; her laughter tempts others to steal her away."

"Maryana," Gable protested, "Are you all right?"

"I am perfectly well, Gable. A little mad with joy at your wedding, that's all." Maryana laughed, her thoughts erasing one profanity of a vision, that of Reverend Valenty, her secret love and torment.

This family parlance was disrupted by the merry invasion of Linda's mother, her very presence domineering. The bride and groom were showered with blessings, and the guests hustled out with hands-full of rice and rose-petals. Finally, when Gable and Linda emerged out into the open night sky studded with stars, they were drowned into tides of fragrance, the clouds of rice and crushed rose-petals settling in their hair and making puddles at their feet. Gable was acting out his role, wedded to his dreams, not to the bride beside him. He was gloating over his own flawless performance and applauding his mastery.

The friends and guests were cheering and following them to their white limousine, but Gable had caught sight of Ethel, and his sense of dream-reality was chilled in the glacier of timelessness. Though cradled in the luxuriant seat of his limousine, hugging his bride, Gable's thoughts were kneeling at the altar of his beloved. Ethel was with him, his heart awakening to the spasms of agony which he thought he had buried deep within. The time itself was the ebb and flow of liquid dreams and formlessness. Visions and shadows were shivering in his head and before his sight His thoughts were swirling into a vortex of pain and elation so overwhelming that he didn't even know how and when he had got into this bridal suite. He sat on a chair unlacing his shoes. Linda stood in a modeling pose, scooping the white silks of her bridal gown in one hand, her other hand poised over the coronet of pearls in her hair.

"How do I look?" Linda's green-gold eyes were radiating the fire of joy.

"Ravishing. Absolutely irresistible." Gable leaped to his feet, catching her into one eager embrace and imprinting mad, feverish kisses upon her lips.

"Have you noticed any change in me?" Linda wiggled out of his arms, gasping for breath.

"You have grown more beautiful, if that is possible

"So, you have not noticed?" Linda pouted.

"Why is laughter fading from your eyes? The change is obvious; you are my sweet, irresistible wife."

"No make-up, you didn't notice? And you are the one who told me you didn't like that mask hiding my face?" Linda chirped, laughter returning in her gaze.

"That's the first thing I noticed. The beauty of your complexion and your beautiful eyes." Gable caught her into his arms once again.

"Do you love me?" Linda swooned, the warmth of his fingers in the process of unbuttoning her gown, racing through her flesh like the crackling of fire.

"Love you?" One agony of a false confession escaped Gable's lips, his heart lurching. "I worship the ground you walk on." He borrowed Aslam's line, his lips sealing hers with kisses hungry and savage.

The night-long orgy of lust and desire had faded into the early hours of dawn, and the ache and longing in Gable's soul were still not sated. Finally, the hands of exhaustion had lulled him to sleep, cradling him into dreams and torments. The demon of lust inside him had retired to its own chamber of sin and darkness, leaving the altar of his beloved exposed to the blasts of changelessness. Ethel was his bride in his dreams

The sunlight glinting through the chinks of heavy drapes had awakened Linda, her heart swollen with joy and love. She lay there, watching her *love of life*, quietly and tenderly. A bleak shadow of sadness crossed suddenly over her features. Her joy was tainted with the sword of a revelation which she dared not hold back or accept. Here was a stranger, lying beside her as her wedded husband. A capricious lover, marked by the brand of lust. A husband who would stay gulfs apart from her in thought and understanding and whom she could not claim as her very own. And yet she could feel his warmth and nearness, and the pulse of her own life throbbing in absolute surrender to her love for this stranger.

Linda dared not stir lest she awaken Gable. She could feel the fury of his kisses on her body, her soul longing for the pain and purity of love, where lust sat supreme. *He did not love her*, this confession alone was a low serenade in her head, challenging her to hug the truth while scattering the seeds of hope. *She would placate his hunger with the feast of her own love until lust was no more*, her thoughts were humming the saddest of tunes in hope and resolve

I will plead with him to confide in me, to share his pain and suffering. He doesn't know how much I love him, now and forever. I will be patient, my love will endure, he will grow to—the scent of sweetness in Linda's thoughts was sucked into the eyes of Gable as he woke up suddenly.

"Where would you like to go on our first day of honeymoon?" Gable asked dreamily.

"Nowhere!" Linda laughed, teasing the island of gold hair on his chest with kisses.

"A great place to be. My favorite." Gable pulled her over to him, his kisses mad and scalding. "Buckets of champagne and bouquets of love, what else does one need? Food perhaps, if we ever get tired of feasting on kisses, and making love until—"

The rod of his desire was plunging into her lotus amidst the throes of her own agony and rapture.

Nine ~ Inception of a Villanelle

The evening hush in the Faulkner's library, because of the musty odor from the books, was quite stifling to Linda. She was seated on a lounge chair by the window, where she could see Gable sleeping on the sofa—a defenseless child who needed great care and affection. It was partly true, since after four months of his marriage he had landed in the hospital on the brink of death. He had suffered a massive heart attack, but triple bypass had worked wonders, and he had almost recovered. It had been almost four weeks since he had returned from the hospital, but he was constrained to rest at home by the orders of the doctor and by the strict vigilance of Linda and of his own mother.

Linda gathered up her green skirt and curled her legs under her as if feeling a sudden chill, her look lingering over Gable in a flood of tenderness. Her own eyes were closing, her heart grateful that Gable's parents had welcomed her as their own daughter and insisting that they stay with them. She was blessed to stay with his parents since she could feel secure and loved by them, if not by the capricious lover as her husband. After his heart attack, she had ceased to be his make-believe bride, or laughing Linda, but a wife in love whose devotion would lend him health and strength. She knew the sickness and paralysis in his soul, but was confident that her love would heal him.

Gable's mother had won her heart, her gentleness and boundless love overwhelming her with awe. She was very fond of Mr. Faulkner, who was contemplative, yet caring. Davie was her favorite. Linda's thoughts were a blissful refrain, *So sweet, so considerate*. He was in love, and he had made her his only confidante, breathing no word of this to any other member of his family, not even to Gable. Maryana was a little reserved, though her visits were short and numbered few. Linda's eyes shot open as if to look through the veil of pain and sadness in Maryana's eyes. She heaved herself up, her gaze resting on the sleeping form of her husband, her heart shuddering to think that he did not love her, that he would not ever fall in love with her. She tiptoed out of the library, seeking the refuge of her own bedroom.

Unloved bride. That's not all, I am barren, too. Heather, in the fifth month of her pregnancy, and Ethel, fourth or …

Gable was pretending to be asleep, knowing exactly when Linda left, but he kept his eyes closed, laying there inert and listless. Within a few weeks of his wedded life he had discovered that Linda was in love with him, and the truth had dawned upon him like a bolt of lightning. What did he expect, a fool that he was, marrying that girl and making love to her like a beast. The memory of that unyielding rage was visiting him even now, but it had lost its sting, confirming his madness to suffer his love for Ethel. Amidst his reveries, Gable heard a car careen into the driveway, and he scrambled up, his heart suddenly thundering.

Ethel and me. We are like two stars confined in one orbit. We are fated to become one sometime, somewhere in this small world, rigged with puzzles and absurdities. Gable strolled toward the window, half thinking, half demurring.

His vision was stung by the purity of this quiet winter evening. The leafless maples capped with snow and the cedars shivering under the weight of glittering whiteness were glaring back at him. A red Pontiac parked at the curb of the driveway was a rude intrusion, its driver emerging forth as a vision of nemesis, no other than Fabian himself. Gable's heart was constricting, longing to have one glimpse of his beloved Ethel who was obviously not accompanying her husband. Almost swaying, Gable returned to his seat of rest, cupping his head into his hands as if driving away the hopelessness. With the whip of his practiced will, he had donned the mask of amenity before Fabian could enter this den of gloom and clutter. Offering his friend the comfort of a rocker, Gable abandoned himself on the sofa opposite him.

"Now that your arteries are unclogged and you have attracted all the attention you didn't deserve, don't you think it high time you got back to work?" Fabian was teasing, assuming the role of an advisor. "Are you done frightening your family and friends? Had I not seen you on the operating table, I would have never believed that you could be a candidate for heart attack. Though, I couldn't help thinking all along that you were feigning this heart attack."

"If feigning illness benefits one's health, then I might cultivate this healthy habit of feigning to improve my health and to gain attention," Gable quipped.

"No invalid have I ever seen so dull and witless like you." Fabian laughed, rubbing his hands for warmth. "Maryana let me in. Where is your laughing bride?"

"I have killed her laughter," Gable said, noticing the confusion in the eyes of his friend.

"What a brute? Have you been unkind to her?" Fabian returned to teasing.

"Unkind only to my own self. Besottedly affectionate toward her, if that's considered unkindness," Gable replied, noticing Maryana's approach, carrying two cups of tea on a small silver tray.

"I told Fabian to wake you up, and he has succeeded already." Maryana handed Gable one cup and turned to offer the other to Fabian.

"Maryana." Fabian claimed the cup. "Didn't notice before, how pale and slim you have grown?"

"The light of the Lord is shining on me," Maryana retorted and literally fled.

"What's wrong with Maryana, Gable? Is she ill?"

"Maladies of the heart and soul, I guess. They kill us, don't they?" Gable intoned.

"How gloomy and morbid your thoughts are, Gable. Do you know that such a state of mind is an atomizer of stress, and if you change not your way of thinking, stress might trigger another heart attack?"

"Would it kill me?" Gable elicited a dry peal of laughter.

"You have certainly gone mad. Entertaining suicidal thoughts, I can tell," Fabian remarked, sipping his tea quietly.

"I am a murderer, isn't it an established fact?" Gable commenced. "And murderers crave to shed more blood. Fortunately, this time I will be the victim of my own brutal instincts."

"If you are intent on romanticizing suicide, then choose a pleasant way of dying." Fabian joined him in his mirth. "The cleanest and daring would be to drown your own self into the depths of Mad River?"

"Death by drowning is not my idea of romanticism," Gable reflected aloud. "Contrary to what I said, I have no intention of dying. The challenges in life have not forsaken me yet, and I am eager to confront them. What are those challenges, I am not sure. Neither do I know what I want and where I'm going? Just exploring the meaningless absurdity in everything that I do. Looking for answers where questions elude me. Looking for something, don't know."

"Hope, you find that *something*, or your way out of that *some thing*?" Fabian's thoughts were suddenly deflated. "Who has the time to look for *something* one doesn't know what?"

"Time is a thing created by simpletons like us," Gable began heedlessly. "In my vocabulary of thoughts, time is a large tunnel inside the vessel of humanity. This vessel inhaling freshness from the bountiful cauldron of nature and exhaling foulness, the tunnel of time bloated by the mingling of odor from humanity and purity from nature. Have you not noticed how time flees from the reek of humanity, yet we force it back into the tunnel of purity and corruption, the former overwhelmed by the latter?

"My sense of smell is not that keen. Only experience and relationships graze my senses, and they are odorless." Fabian breathed unconvincingly.

"The defecations of time and humanity do not reach you, how fortunate. Only the scent of roses and lilacs." Gable stopped, noticing the approach of his mother.

"You are supposed to be lying down, Gable, not sitting." Mrs. Faulkner shot an apprehensive look at her son. "Fabian won't mind if you rested your head on the pillow while talking and enjoying his company." Her eyes were flashing. "Linda told me you have not been behaving lately, and she is coming right down to check on you."

"Two tyrants to watch over me at all times, Mom. You and Linda, of course," Gable chirped with a mingling of blithe and mischief. "Wish, it was possible to employ Maryana as my nurse and employer?"

"Man, indeed, is ungrateful. I got to be going." Fabian sprang to his feet.

"You don't have to leave, Fabian. Besides, I haven't spoken with you yet." Mrs. Faulkner urged him to sit down. "Where is Ethel?"

"She has gone to a bridge party." Fabian maintained his lie, unwilling to share the news of her pregnancy in front of Gable.

"Seems like we're going to have a party." Linda sailed into the room, catching only the last word from Fabian's lips. "You can't stay though, Gable has not been resting as advised by the doctors, and he must suffer the penalty."

"I am leaving, only detained by your kind mother-in-law." Fabian laughed.

"You must stay for dinner, it's almost ready," Linda appealed, her warm gaze enfolding all into a cloak of love and sunshine.

"Thank you, but I can't. Ethel should be home soon. Goodbye," Fabian said as he turned to leave.

"I will see you to the door, and then check on dinner." Mrs. Faulkner followed him, leaving behind her tender smiles with Linda and Gable.

"I feel so tired suddenly," Gable mumbled, his look wearied.

"Will tuck you in bed right after you eat your dinner," Linda teased, abandoning herself on the sofa beside him.

"Without you, I can't sleep, my dear." Gable wound his arms around her waist, holding her to himself.

"Will lie down with you, 'til you fall asleep," Linda said sweetly.

"Might not sleep untill dawn," Gable teased back.

Gable had spent half the night making love to Linda. Finally, when he had dozed off, his dreams were the marshlands of his own lusts, hungers, and appetites. The day had emerged forth glittering, the treetops threaded with beads of snow and reflecting rainbow of colors in a flood of sunshine. After a cozy lunch with Linda in the bedroom, he was permitted to indulge in the pleasure of writing before it was time to rest again. Linda had left him with a tablet of commandments, allotting him no more than half an hour of writing at one stretch, interspersed with intervals of rest and exercise. But Gable, seated at his cherry desk and writing feverishly, had grown oblivious to time or commandments. His thoughts alone were his guide, whether sweeping over the papers in a hurricane of words, or exploring the labyrinths in his psyche inside the hush of fever and silence.

The swirling downpour from his thoughts was truncated abruptly, his sight reaching out to the scenic chill in nature where it could be seen through the frame of his bedroom window. He could see the frozen beads of ice lit by the shafts of sunshine, as if the naked limbs of the trees were haloed by some holy dance of fire and sparkle in nature. An overwhelming sense of wonder was seething his chilled awareness, the shining abyss within him growing dark. The reek of his own lust and despair were invading his senses, the altar of his love for Ethel defiled and desecrated.

Linda, the victim of my lust and madness, and she loves me. One blister of a thought in Gable's head was unzipping its foul lips. *I try to be good and loving, don't I? But all is nightmare, this brand of destiny carving dark hopes that Ethel and I will be united—soon, forever.* His thoughts were pulsating with the rhythm of life and living torment. *I am a fool, an utter dolt, fit to be drowned inside some pit of fire and contempt.*

"Let me sleep in peace, wake me up on Judgment Day." His pen was ready to fly, but inspiration had fled his thoughts.

Gable didn't even notice that Linda had returned. She had stolen behind him and was looking over his shoulders, censoring his script with her eyes alone.

"Such a downpour of doom and gloom, Gable. You have forfeited the right to write from now on," Linda declared abruptly, her heart sinking.

"My dear." Gable was jolted out of his dark reveries. "There is no gloom in my thoughts, but negation," he replied, stretching his arms over his shoulders and pulling her closer to him without stirring or turning.

"Your dark contemplations, Gable, they don't make any sense to me." Linda closed her eyes, grazing her lips against the thatch of gold on his head.

"A beautiful façade to shield your intellect, isn't it? Why, I don't know?" Gable got to his feet and stood facing her. "Your intellect is much too refined; you can't hide it from me. What you think as the bullet of doom and gloom is nothing but the inception of a villanelle. I composed the entire villanelle in my sleep, but all is gone except this one line. I will probably not add another line to it." He went over to the window, looking out, his back toward her.

"Poetry is therapeutic. You should complete your villanelle," Linda urged unconvincingly.

"How I detest poetry," Gable said. "Well, I shouldn't say that." His tone was tinged with remorse. "I like reading poetry, not writing it. I prefer prose. Somehow, it feels more solid, muscular, man-thing. Poetry is feminine, demanding—don't know what I am saying."

"Time to rest, Gable. After that you'll know what you want to say," Linda coaxed.

"No, it's not." Gable whirled around to face her. "Two hours and twenty minutes on my disposal still, exactly." He looked at the watch on his wrist, frowning to himself. "You have become a tyrant, Linda, do you know?" He smiled, gazing into her eyes thoughtfully. "Rest is not what I need, but activity. Mental activity, if you spare me the mockery of your gaze." He returned to the seat at his desk and grabbed the pen.

"I will sit in bed and read, if you don't mind?" Linda snatched the pile of papers which Gable had abandoned beside the bedside table and plopped herself down.

"Your pleasure, love," Gable said over his shoulders, his fingers already moving on the page in long, fierce strokes.

"May I read what you have written so far?" Linda was intent on reading, propping a pillow behind her head.

"As long as you don't laugh out loud."

"Don't promise anything." Linda shot back.

Ethel, Ethel. He loves her. Linda's thoughts were repeating this phrase. The script in her hand was fading from her sight like the dewdrops scorched to nothingness. *I thought he would forget. Am I going mad? Yes. Gable is mad, too. Madness attracts madness. We are all mad, me, him, his family. Davie and Maryana. All of us, Ethel and Fabian—*her disjointed thoughts were disrupted by Mr. Faulkner's loud voice.

"Come down, Gable, Bryan is here to see you."

Gable added another line to his villanelle before leaping to his feet. *My wearied and restless soul cries in plea.* Flashing a quick glance at Linda, he scurried out of the room. Down in the parlor, Bryan had made himself comfortable on the sofa. Gable sat in the chair opposite.

"A few minutes and then you can go back to your lair of writing," Bryan announced.

"That means you would be imposing for hours," Gable quipped.

"Honestly, I can't stay long." Bryan laughed. "Though I am an agent of wrath, to sweep the entire world of news into a fistful of ashes, but I won't begin this charitable task until I make sure that my invalid friend is on the road to recovery

"Linda would put your invalid friend to bed if your visit exceeded the limit of half an hour." Gable replied.

"She should be awarded a medal for taming you thus." Bryan's humor was uncontrollable. "How is your novel coming along?"

"Every time I finish a chapter I have this wild impulse to burn the whole thing." But then something inside me checks my madness, and I stay tune to the fever of writing."

"I will kindle a lusty blaze for you, if you want." Bryan chuckled.

"I'm sure," Gable said. "But I won't give you the satisfaction of gloating over the blight of my works, no matter how worthless they are."

"What gloom sits in your eyes?" Bryan asked. "Well, all married men have this affliction, perhaps?"

"Don't gloat over your freedom, Bryan," Gable began amusedly. "I have a feeling you'll be tying the knot of marriage soon, and this is a prophecy."

"Don't prophesy, my friend. Prophecies tend to lean toward tragedies." Bryan was getting serious and contemplative.

"If you consider marriage a tragedy," Gable responded.

"An interesting topic for discussion, but it would require buckets of time to douse the arguments into some pool of sensibility." Bryan got to his feet. "True to my promise, I must leave—go pound the news to dust. When are you coming back to work?"

"Soon, I'm hoping." Gable said as fatigue and weariness began to show.

"Goodbye." Bryan shook Gable's hand and scuttled away.

Gable couldn't move. How long did he sit there in this state of immobility, he had no recollection, only vaguely aware that Linda had urged him to lie down on the couch, tucking him under a soft blanket. He had dozed off, drifting into the valley of his inner loneliness. Hope was there, knitting the cloak of sanity. This rhythm of silence was splintered by a peal of laughter. Linda had brought coffee, and Aslam and Heather had materialized from nowhere.

"This healthy lout is enjoying extraordinary privileges at home." Aslam was teasing Linda. "When is he returning back to work?"

"Leave my husband alone. He is working perfectly well at home." Linda's laughter was enveloping all. "One more week, and he is back to the grinding mill of labor for living, as you call it."

"She is the commander of my fate. A merciless general." Gable could not help but be a part of these inanities which had landed upon him from the ether, it seemed.

"Shame on you, Aslam," Heather chimed in. "How clever of you to divert our attention from the joke you were telling. It's a man-thing, I guess, to start something and never finish. Nothing is shocking to our ears, I assure you. We are not school-girls."

"Doctors can never be careful enough." Aslam smiled at his wife. "This joke might taint our child's innocence?" He shifted his appeal to Linda.

"Let's leave these men to their own vices of stealth and corruption." Linda waved pontifically, turning her attention to Heather. "We would be comfortable in the library." She got to her feet. "I have to show you the new books I got." She claimed Heather's hand, and they ambled away laughing.

"If the air gets stifling up there, you are welcome to our den of vices," Gable tossed this comment after them. Turning to Aslam, "I hear the prospect of being a father fills one with a sense of pride and power."

"Don't feel that way." Aslam laughed. "Though I am already jealous of the child. Who would claim Heather's love while I would fade away into nothingness?"

"The child inside you is intolerable, I guess," Gable said.

"The child in all of us," Aslam declared. "The child inside you remains defiant, demanding something which belongs to someone else. You know what I mean."

"Ethel," Gable said.

"Yes. No doubt," Aslam replied.

"Some sort of absurdity compels me to believe that Ethel and I are destined to be together," Gable began. "How, why, and when I don't know. Fate has decreed thus, and fates can't be altered or averted, as the Greeks say."

"Greeks are the ones who perfected the religion for all eternity, all lunatics say, and you are on the road to be initiated into that circle." Aslam breathed intensely. "Though, you look sane when Linda is around. My observation is that you have fallen in love with your own wife."

"A love most impoverished if it feeds itself on the crumbs of affection alone."

"The warmth of affection gives birth to love," Aslam said.

"It breeds only pity, never kindling the fire of love." Gable responded.

"Love is something elusive, just like your dream, or absurdity in hoping beyond hope," Aslam began thoughtfully. "Would you rather dream away your life in pursuit of love which you can't possess, or learn to love what you have?"

"Reality and illusion are relative terms. What is reality for one might be an illusion to the other," Gable remarked unconvincingly. "As long as my dream goads me to follow, I would not abandon it. The shadow of pain is my only bridge of reality."

"My only fear is, your heart would not contain all that pain, and stress." Aslam's tone was apprehensive. "You are a prime candidate for another heart attack if you refuse to learn how to handle your stress."

"You mean my pain." Gable smiled. "I would survive; the lips of fate have told me so."

"I mean, hold on to the hem of your affection for Linda. How deep is your affection?"

"Affection has no depths, you moron, it is always shallow," Gable said.

"*Always,* a terrible word." Aslam caught a sparkle in his friend's eyes. "Even shallow has degrees of depths in its shallowness. Your own lunacy in hope and survival would not carry you far."

"Any cure for such madness?" Gable challenged.

"A prescription full of bitter antidotes ...." Aslam could not continue, noticing the breezy return of Linda and Heather.

"Sorry to disrupt your delicious meal of conversation, but it's time to leave." Heather appealed to Aslam. "Nothing to worry, but I feel a little giddy and nauseous."

"It is my duty to worry about you, love." Aslam stood, slipping his arm around her waist.

"I had hoped you would stay for dinner, but ...." Linda left her thoughts unuttered.

"Thank you, but we won't let you off that easy. Would be back next week, if not earlier," Aslam teased. "Goodbye. No need to chase us to the door." He laughed, noticing Gable scramble to his feet.

Linda and Gable, after waving goodbye to their friends at the front door and watching their car roll out of the driveway, returned to the parlor in utter silence. Both were feeling some sort of chill and emptiness, as if warmth had been sucked out of their home and hearth. Gable flung himself upon the sofa while Linda had settled herself on the rocker near the fireplace, watching the smoldering of flames and embers.

"Do you believe in fate, Linda?" Gable asked abruptly.

"Only, if it holds a promise of fortunes in my favor"

"Watch out, my dear, it might deceive you, its favors hidden into a pot of misfortunes." Gable looked deep into the emerald brilliance of her eyes as if searching for something.

"Do authors get paid for such trite expressions?" Linda chirped mirthfully.

"Only, if they get a chance to act out their lives in the stream of banality," Gable said. "This house seems so strange today, even your voice and laughter? Wonder, why? Probably since no one is around? Maryana is not coming home this evening, I suppose."

"No. She's in seclusion after her ceremony of initiation," Linda said, laughter fading from her eyes. "It's rather chilly today, but the house feels the same. Quiet, but not strange. I don't think so."

"Haven't seen Davie for days. Music is gone from here; don't you miss it?"

"Carnegie Hall is his second home now, but he's scheduled to fly back tomorrow," Linda consoled. "Let's eat. Food would pour some warmth into your body and thoughts."

"It would be a special treat if we could eat here?" Gable closed his eyes. "I feel tired suddenly."

"You'd be treated to a warm bed right here, too. And don't fall asleep before I fetch food."

Many savory dinners and hours of rest in the comfort of his own bedroom every night seemed like a dream to Gable as he sat writing at his desk. Suddenly, he was becoming aware of the wind beating at the windows and the snow falling in swirling madness. The cold, wild blasts outside were entering his own thoughts, awakening him to the threshold of remorse that Linda had been sitting on the couch reading and that he had not spoken a word since hours. Feeling the sting of his own selfishness, he kicked his chair back and stood facing his much-neglected wife.

"I have been acting like a selfish colt for the past few days, haven't I?" Gable announced.

"Have you?" Linda lifted her eyes off the book, as if startled.

"Don't know? You tell me." Gable said.

"Not selfish, but childish, if you ask me." Linda smiled. "Insisting on writing for hours, neglecting your rest, and doing everything contrary to the advice of your doctor."

"No truth to all these accusations. I do rest and I have a great appetite. What I was trying to say I get so absorbed in writing that I tend to neglect you. Unintentionally, of course, and I feel guilty."

"You may neglect me as much as you like as long as you succeed in finishing your novel," Linda encouraged, half mocking, half appealing.

"That would be the day. Never, it seems." Gable replied. "What do I smell? Something delicious and appetizing!" He inhaled deeply, his keen senses absorbing the aroma of cooking. "Who's coming to dinner?"

"A special family dinner. How you forget, Gable," Linda chided sweetly. "A special dinner in honor of your getting back to work tomorrow?"

"Yes, how could I forget? My family doing their best to celebrate my exile from freedom." Gable drifted toward the door. "I need to talk with Davie before mother commands me, or us, to the dining room." He stalked out.

Linda sat listless for a few minutes and then plodded toward the desk where Gable's writing lay exposed to her scrutiny.

Let me sleep in peace, wake me up on Judgment Day

My wearied and restless soul cries in plea

All thoughts are dunes of sand, and mind a pot of clay—

Her thoughts gathered each word like a brand of fire. She stood suspended, absorbed deep in her reflections, oblivious to time or surroundings. Down in the parlor, Gable had forgotten about Linda and about his writing, urging Davie to play, if not goading him into arguments.

"How divinely you are playing this evening, Davie." Gable sat applauding. "Are you in love?"

"Yes. With my music." Davie said.

"This love so boundless, that you can share with the world." Gable beamed. "But that's not the kind of love I'm talking about, and you know what I mean, so spill it out." He prodded.

"Whatever I spill won't reach you since you are sitting a mile away from me." Davie wheeled his chair back. "Music is my love that is true. My wedded bride. How can I divorce her and seek another?" he asked.

"So, you're not going to reveal the name of your true love to your brother, that much is obvious." Gable heaved a mock sigh, settling himself on the chair beside him. "And yet my curiosity goads me to ask, who is the lucky girl?"

"What an insufferable prig you are, Gable." Davie laughed, his heart unwilling to unfold the sanctity of his secret. "You are deluded in thinking that I am in love. Another grand delusion of yours to keep you imprisoned inside the walls of delusion."

"Delusion doesn't arrest our imagination, my sage brother, but liberates us to explore the labyrinths of truth forbidden and truth forgotten," Gable replied. "A first rung toward the temple of discovery."

"You and your epigrams, Gable, no one understands them. Spare me the profundity of your thoughts."

"You are right, I am an insufferable prig," Gable admitted cheerfully. "Didn't even congratulate you on your recent performance at Carnegie Hall. You make us all proud, congratulations. Now, be an angel, and play something wild and fantastic. I'm in a mood for riot. Tchaikovsky, if you don't mind. My favorite, but when *you* play, it makes the mountains soar to the sky."

"Must pay the price of your flattery before mom hauls us to the dining room." Davie spun his chair back to the piano, his fingers caressing the black and ivory keys.

The violence of music rose in a sudden crescendo, as Gable closed his eyes. The knots of pain inside him were snapping loose and cutting through the thin fabric of his soul. A cold, cold tomb inside him was lifting its slab of silence, whispering to him one terrible secret. He had failed—failed most wretchedly in his attempt to cease loving Ethel. The void of pain and silence inside him was swallowed by the surge and violence of music rippling aloft. His eyes opened abruptly as Maryana's voice reached his silence.

"Your heathenish music is making mom nervous, Davie. Besides, you have a call from New York. We should hook the phone to your chair." Davie wheeled out of the room in utmost haste.

"You have lost ear for music, Maryana," Gable lamented.

"Wish you could look into your eyes this moment, Gable." Maryana said. "So much pain and hopelessness. What are you thinking?"

"Does one always have to think? Can't one sit idle and not think?" Gable averted her stare. "Can't bear to look at you, Maryana. You have grown so pale. Don't you trust me anymore? You are suffering, I know, but—"

"You have mastered the art of evasion, Gable. My pallor has nothing to do with any kind of suffering, but with my recent illness. Didn't tell you because you would've worried yourself sick, but I am fine now," Maryana expounded. "You are the one suffering, not even admitting that you do. Just asked you what you were thinking and you can't even tell me that."

"It is better to keep my thoughts to myself to preserve the purity of your mind," Gable replied.

"My mind is not as pure as you think," Maryana said.

"I was thinking about Ethel."

"Nothing wrong in thinking about her. She's your friend."

"She is my *hope*, my *sanity*. I worship her, cannot live without her." Gable's voice was a cry.

"You shouldn't say such things, much less think about them," Maryana said.

"I have frightened you, forgive me," Gable apologized. "What a beast I ...." He couldn't continue, noticing his mother sailing towards them.

"What beasts?   Don't scare your mother."   Mrs. Faulkner approached slowly. "Dinner is ready, and your father is getting impatient, better hurry."

"Dad would eat us alive if he didn't get his food on time." Gable sprang to his feet, laughing.

Ten ~ Love Desecrated

The balmy summer evening was teasing the ache and longing in Gable's heart. He sat with his friends on the front lawn of his parents' home trying his best to add joy to this special occasion. This was the eve of his parents wedding anniversary. They had been married for thirty years. This evening celebrations were mainly arranged by Gable and Linda, though Davie and Maryana had contributed much of their time in planning and writing invitations. The lawn was brimming with guests. Davie's musician friends were playing a medley of tunes to entertain the Faulkners and their friends, as well as the younger groups invited by Gable and Linda.

Four uneventful years had marched past with astonishing haste since Gable's heart attack, and he had learned to live with the agony of inner void. This void was Gable's only link to sanity, that his love for Ethel would find fulfillment in the end by some invisible bolt of magic. No magic had come to his rescue. Ethel had become the mother of a lovely daughter who was now a three-year-old and had become the pinnacle of his love and adoration. Kimberly was the name of this child with blue eyes and flaxen hair who had claimed Gable's heart as if she was his own daughter. As soon as this thought of Kimberly crossed Gable's mind a pang of ice shot through his awareness.

No one could conceive of a platonic relationship in marriage, but Lord Byron. Gable's thoughts were running to his defense as he stood watching the purity of dusk. *Why did I think that my beloved would remain a virgin bride all her life?* He was becoming aware of the faces and voices, his steps guiding him involuntarily.

The wheels of fate, with hope as their leverage, were churning in Gable's head. He had mounted the first rung of success by finishing his novel, *Children of God*, but the ladder had been pulled out from under him before he could aim for the next. True, that his novel was published, a few thousand copies sold, but the disdain and the mockery of the reviewers has left him bitter and isolated. He was feeling isolated amidst this throng of friends too, his gaze catching sight of Maryana, her eyes the pools of serenity.

She looks blissful, utterly at peace with herself and with the world. So white, so peaceful, so beautiful, but this is not Maryana, she looks like one who has surrendered herself to death.

He was mingling with the guests, talking and laughing, yet drifting like a ghost. The ghastly chamber of silence inside him was parading a vision, that of Linda. He was a part of that vision, both waiting for some gong of battle which could provoke a clash for better or worse. His gaze was alighted on Davie, the icon of repose and salubrity. To him, Davie was a confident chess-king. Waiting for all his subjects to die while defending him so that he could be left alone with his queen.

His eyes had caught a glimpse of his beloved. Ethel was standing a few paces away from him amidst the company of her friends, her beauty outshining Venus. Gable could neither move, nor think, his look glazed. He was lost in the bliss of oblivion, not even noticing that Maryana had stolen behind him. She was now standing beside him, her gaze tracing his own, and then returning to him.

"Isn't it odd Gable that you are standing here all by yourself while your friends are making merry and feasting?" Maryana chided with a mingling of challenge and tenderness. "Don't you find it absurd?" She asked, as he turned to face her.

"Pleasant absurdities, my dear, they feed my soul," Gable responded.

"I am hoping and praying, Gable, that such absurdities of yours don't spoil the evening for mom and dad," Maryana warned, stricken by the ocean of pain in her brother's eyes. "Bryan has been looking for you, where were you? Come, let me leave you in his care, I will feel comfortable if he stays with you. You are not listening, Gable! Do I have to throw a noose around your neck and drag you?" She snatched his hand into hers, which felt hot and moist. "You have fever, Gable, and you don't even know. You must lie down."

"Don't be a fool, Maryana. Your hand is cold." Gable pressed her cold fingers before releasing. "My body temperature is perfectly normal, and I don't feel feverish." He laughed. "There is fever in my soul, if that's a satisfactory explanation."

"That fever is burning through your flesh, and you are ill Gable," Maryana muttered helplessly.

"I feel wonderful. Much healthier than I have ever felt before," Gable replied. "This sense of power and invulnerability inside me, it's new and exhilarating. It feels as if I can conquer the heavens if I put my mind to it?" He lit a cigarette.

"How many times your doctor has told you not to smoke, Gable?" Maryana reminded him. "Your friend Aslam advises you to do the same?"

"Aslam, the arbiter of my fate." Gable kept smoking. "Where is that prophet of health? I haven't seen him this evening."

"I thought I told you? Fabian brought the happy news. Aslam is the father of a girl, born this very afternoon. Now, a proud father of two, I should say."

"No one told me, Maryana. You disappeared after breakfast, God knows where," Gable said.

"You don't seem happy by this." Maryana heaved a sigh of relief as Bryan appeared like a changeling and dragged Gable away.

"We are having a serious discussion, and we need your witless participation," Bryan said. "I have been arguing with this dolt of a philosopher for the past fifteen minutes about the reality of life and death, and he doesn't get my point." He flashed a challenge at Fabian.

"Where is the jest behind this comedy of arguments?" Gable asked.

"If you listen to what Bryan said, a laughing jest would grab you by the neck," Fabian responded. "In his estimation, this present life is death and death itself in true essence the font of life. Imagine if we were to sing, Oh, *sweet ecstasies of white death, you awaken us to the light of utter happiness. Oh, agonies of dark life, you confound our senses in this pit of non-existence.*" He laughed.

"How many glasses of beer and how many goblets of wine. You are positively drunk, my friend." Gable answered. "You are making no sense. Sages and saints have tried to enlighten us about the reality of life and death for ages, but does anyone understand? Not even the masters of profundity, I am sure. A reversal of names, perhaps. To name life, death, won't rob life of its breath, nor would it awaken the silence of death to life."

"You are not as ignorant as you pretend to be?" Bryan responded.

"How can I be guilty of this noble pretense when I don't even know what you are talking about?" said Gable. "Life and death, this paradox. Our puny minds are not equipped for *understanding*. How does your intellect dissect this paradox? Go ahead, shoot your ideas."

"Ideas unlock the grave of truth, if one contemplates," Bryan began promptly. "What we call life is nothing but a phantom of illusions. Shadows drifting and shuffling on the canvas of nothingness, beyond which rests the essence of everything. Death, as the womb and tomb of life, churning the reflections of continuity, where we see ourselves as the victims or spectators of joy, pain, struggle, uncertainty, while remaining blind to the cosmic wholeness of love and unity in time and timelessness."

"Am I the only one buried alive into this sea of imponderables?" Fabian waved his arm in a gesture of hopelessness.

"Paradoxically, stupidity and arrogance rule our thoughts." Gable turned his attention to Bryan. "And we don't have the courage to pound our thoughts to dust to rise above the dung of words, ideas, presumptions."

"Would it be a mark of courage to proclaim love as hate, and hate as love?" Fabian was still caught inside the whirlpool of his own *brand-name* meaning of words.

"It would be interesting, if not courageous, I guess." Bryan's eyes were lit up with the sparks of fresh animation. "The passion of hatred is nobler than that of love in terms of its purity and perseverance. Hatred is the fire which feeds the furnace of life, ever constant, ever blazing, and gaining success in its own field of power and possession. While love is the pulse of weakness, faithless and inconstant, dying with each breath, and failing in its mission to discover the mystery of its own passion. Hate conquers and love surrenders. Hate is strength, love is impotence. Hate is closer to reality, love farther from truth. Now tell me, which one is noble?"

"A choice between lunacy and dementia, a noble and difficult decision," Fabian mocked.

"Passionately speaking, a choice between, when one hates to love, and loves to hate," Bryan replied.

"In favor of passionate evidence, you have fallen in love with so many girls at the same time that the novelty of your passion is drained out of your romantic guts," Gable expounded. "Now that the girls have unmasked your propensity at play, they don't call you after being jilted, laughing behind your back. Quite a blow to your ego, isn't it?"

"Atrociously misjudged, I plead, *Not Guilty*." Bryan laughed. "I am truly in love, now and forever, with Ann. Though, she treats me cruelly, making fun of my love."

"At least, she listens to the most acclaimed liar of this century?" Fabian teased.

"I would rather she was deaf," Bryan cried in despair. "At least, then, if she rejected my love, I would be consoled that she couldn't endure the flood of my anguish and devotion."

"You would act out your part even then, Bryan, and she would see the corruption inside your heart I am sure," Gable said.

"All these unkind and unjust remarks. I don't think I deserve such treatment," Bryan protested. "My love is pure, tainted only by longings. If I could only explain how a fire rises inside me like one giant blaze."

"When was this fire kindled? A week ago," Gable retorted, becoming aware of Linda and Ethel sailing toward them.

"How selfish to make an exclusive circle of your own and abandon your wife." Ethel stood facing Fabian, her eyes shining with mock accusations. "Everyone else is enjoying their dinner, and I am hoping you would join me."

"My appetite might improve if I didn't sit with you." Linda was seeking Gable's attention, but he was watching Ethel.

Gable said, "Here, join us in our appetizing discussion of —"

"No appetizers before dinner, I am starving." Was Ethel's sing-song response, as she turned to Linda. "Let's flee before our hunger is spoiled by the odor of their jargon."

"I wonder, if it's a curse or a blessing to be guided by women," Bryan chanted.

"Get married, and you would find the answer," Linda commented, stealing a glance at Gable before she followed Ethel.

The evening had drifted into night, the sky wearing a lace of stars and the moon all radiant. Gable had stayed with his friends, talking and laughing. He had heaped his plate like the rest of his friends, but had no idea what he was eating, only aware that he was drinking more than he could contain. His thoughts were restless, following his beloved wherever she went. Even while returning to the circle of his friends with his plate laden with food, he was suspended in worshipful reverie, gazing at Ethel where she sat eating amongst her friends. Now sated and drunk, he sat with his friends, caught inside the hurricane of words.

"Yesterday, I was a lover," Bryan was saying, "today I'm a fool, and tomorrow I would conquer my follies. Why look mournful, Gable, when the night is alive and studded with stars?"

"You are babbling like a fool, for sure. Wine has gone to your head, don't you think?" Gable asked. "The last time I saw you in such a state of giddiness was when you were abandoned by two girlfriends two days in a row."

"Isn't my giddiness much more pleasant than your mournfulness?" Bryan chuckled. "I feel light and stupid, I admit."

"My sympathies," Gable murmured, his eyes riveted to his beloved.

"You should congratulate me rather than offer sympathies. Nothing makes sense in this world, does it? A maze of absurdities. A cauldron of contradictions," Bryan said.

Davie and his friends had struck the tunes of the *Polonaise*, and Gable could feel as if Chopin himself was teasing the strings of his inner torment. His eyes were still riveted on Ethel. A volley of applause broke forth, as everyone began to clap, chanting both requests and felicitations.

Gable had seen Ethel rise to her feet, clapping with a wild abandon, her white face radiant and glowing. He heaved himself up, his feet guiding him to the altar of his love. He was drifting toward dream-oblivion, watching the hands of *destiny* challenging the temple of *fate*. Ethel was his temple and goddess, his *bride* of the *night*, veiled in stars. His very soul was on fire, a blaze of longings, which thirsted only for the wine of *love* on the brink of death. He thought he was carried to the heavens, beyond stars and galaxies, not even knowing that a sudden blow had sent him reeling to the ground in one ludicrous heap.

Eleven ~ Invalid at Heart

Where am I? Gable's eyes were opening amidst the fogs of dreams. *How long I have slept? Where is Linda?* The shock and horror of his *madness* on the eve of his parents' wedding anniversary was unfolding in his thoughts like a brand of shame and agony. *Beloved*—the sweetness of kisses which he had tasted then, was now scorching his lips with the dregs of bitterness and damnation.

Gable was becoming aware of the silence in his bedroom. He was grinding his teeth as if ready to cut the wound of desecration on his lips. A volcano of pain was erupting inside his soul with such savage assault that his body was jerked up to a sitting position, involuntarily. Maryana appeared in the bedroom like an apparition, but he sat still in his bed, watching her.

"So glad you are up, Gable." Maryana said. "You will make me very happy if you eat this soup. It's hot and delicious." She held out the soup bowl, as if entreating a child.

"Ethel is never going to forgive me." Gable groaned, claiming the steaming bowl.

"Hush, Gable, hush," Maryana consoled softly. "Just finish your soup, you need strength and nourishment."

"I can't. I am suddenly nauseous." Gable edged closer to the bed and set the soup bowl on the side table.

"Because your stomach is empty. You need to force yourself to swallow a couple of spoons."

"What happened? Was it last night? A nightmare? No, don't tell me," Gable murmured feverishly, his eyes closed. "How long has it been? It seems, I have been lying in my bed for months? Tell your base, wretch of a brother, a coward that he is—"

"You suffered a mild heart attack." Maryana shuddered visibly. "Not months, but only a week! Two days in the hospital, and then home. No major damage to your heart, but you have been delirious." She continued, as if talking to herself. "Mom and dad have sat with you for hours, but obviously you don't remember. Bryan came to see you too, but you've been sleeping most of the time."

"Where's Linda?" Gable asked feebly.

"She is visiting her friends in Indiana," Maryana offered reluctantly.

"She has left me, you mean." Gable demurred aloud, his heart aching.

"Don't say a word, Gable, just rest. No need to entertain such gloomy thoughts." Maryana elicited one pale smile.

"Where is Davie?" Gable asked heedlessly.

"In New York. Hustling his way through a succession of concerts," Maryana said.

"So Adonis is serenading his Phoebe?" Gable declared with a stab at humor.

"Who is Phoebe?" Maryana asked.

"Some beautiful goddess of song and beauty, whom Davie wishes to marry."

"You are raving again, Gable. Why don't you close your eyes and try to empty your mind of all thoughts?" Maryana suggested.

"Yes. Can't forget how despicably I behaved that evening?" Gable groaned. "Linda is right in leaving me, I deserve it. I am unworthy, even of her hate and disgust." His thoughts were becoming incoherent.

"Stop tormenting yourself, Gable," Maryana insisted. "Get yourself some rest and I'll be back with a huge menu of your choice. What would you like to eat?"

"Stuffed flounder."

"You better stuff your head with good thoughts if you want that special treat." Maryana waved a warning before plodding out of his room.

Two whole weeks since Gable's casual remark about stuffed flounder had forced him to stuff his stomach and his recovery was miraculous from then on, effacing all traces of self-pity and the sense of unworthiness. This evening, he was sitting alone in the parlor, leafing through the pages of Time Magazine, more for the sake of occupation, than for reading. A feeling of utter languor had taken hold of him. His eyes were closing, seeking the smoothness of dewdrop memories where pains were silent.Gable's back was pressed against the hefty cushions, his eyes closed and his head tilted to one side. In his mind's vision, he was hurled headlong toward some lonely island where silence was imbedded with thorns of memories unforgettable. This desert of silence was revealing an altar high, the monument of grief. Here was a place most holy and he could see himself kneeling at the very feet of his beloved, shedding tears of penance, and praying for forgiveness. A whiff of breeze, was ruffling his hair, and he could see his own tears and pallor in the mirror of dreams and reflections. His eyes shot open. Gable's mother had materialized, comfortably installed on the lounge opposite from where he sat.

"Mom," Gable whispered. "You are such a comfort and blessing to me, Mom, do you know that? Considering, my follies bring you so much pain and heartache." He was leaving the valley of his grief. "Where is dad?"

"He's becoming a slave of his habits." Mrs. Faulkner smiled. "Taking a nap before dinner has become his religious duty." Her gentle humor was guiding her to console and comfort him.

"Dad. He loses his temper so quickly. But he is all gentleness when Maryana is around. Where is she? Haven't seen her for three whole days?" Gable let his thoughts ramble, as if speaking to himself.

"Maryana," Mrs. Faulkner said. "I'm worried about her. She has grown so pale. Looks … unhappy."

"Couldn't help notice that myself. That sad, distant look in her eyes," Gable replied. "I told her, had she not been a nun, I would have thought she was in love?"

"No wonder, she deems you incorrigible. How could you say that?" Mrs. Faulkner asked.

"Any news from Linda?" Gable asked evasively.

"She's staying with her parents," Mrs. Faulkner began reluctantly. "I thought dad told you, she has filed for divorce?"

"No, dad didn't tell me." Gable was crushed by the shadow of pain in his mother's eyes. "Sorry, Mom. I wish, she could forgive, could come back."

"We wish that too." Mrs. Faulkner was looking out of the window, watching the red Pinto slide into the driveway. "You have a visitor." She got to her feet. "Will let him in and go check on dinner." She smiled at Gable before plodding out of the room.

Gable, too, had seen the visitor. Aslam was quick to turn off the engine, slamming the door shut after he got out of his Pinto. In a flash, Aslam had invaded the parlor, making himself at home, and grinning at Gable with his familiar air of mischief.

"So, how is my invalid friend?" Aslam was teasing. "It's such a gloomy evening. I should have gone home instead of visiting the healthy deceiver."

"I don't see any signs of regret on your face in making this decision to visit me," Gable quipped. "It's obvious you are dying to know when I'm getting back to work. This invalid deceiver is scheduled to start work, bright and early tomorrow. With your permission, of course."

"You don't appreciate the time and favor of an overworked physician who should be sitting home with his lovely wife and adorable kids," Aslam retorted. "Actually, I wanted to make sure you *are* going back to work tomorrow. You are fit as a fiddle. Fortunately, no damage done to your heart. The symptoms of cardiac arrest turned out to be false. You just fizzled out under the assault of shock and delirium. You knew that, didn't you, and you were expecting me to explain."

"Expecting—not explanations. But expecting, someone, something, always waiting and expecting," Gable mumbled enigmatically.

"If you were waiting for a train to go nowhere, I wouldn't be worried. But, I can guess what or who you are waiting for and that's dangerous. You should stop thinking about … you know what I mean? Stress is poison to your heart, and you must stay away from it. Write another book. Your first one, fifteen hundred copies sold, isn't that encouraging? The art of expressing your thoughts on paper is therapeutic. Cling to it with all your might and you would stay healthy. The word, catharsis, as you are so fond of using, is your vaccine for health, not only for your mind, but for your body."

"Isn't it fortunate that doctors can't inject catharsis with a needle, or they would be hurting a lot of their patients," Gable said. "What do you know about catharsis, or about its healing qualities, it doesn't fit into the jargon of your scientific knowledge."

"I know enough, and I know someone who is deprived of this healing potion, such as catharsis, and is suffering terribly," Aslam responded thoughtfully.

"Someone very dear to you, it seems." Gable responded.

"My sister," Aslam said.

"Is she ill?" Gable asked.

"Her husband thinks she is." Aslam elicited one thin smile. "To me, she is perfectly healthy. In fact, she is a paragon of health, except for her dark moods. And those moods are the result of a famine in her mind, so common with any normal or sensitive person deprived of *food* for *thought*."

"This ethereal statement doesn't fit your scientific mold. What do you mean?" Gable watched his friend with a mingling of concern and incredulity.

"Scientific world treats her with respect, telling her she is sane. But her husband tells her she is going crazy." Aslam's expression was moody. "Catharsis, remember, that's where this word comes into play. My sister is a poetess, and writing is her need and food for sustenance. She has no time for this need or luxury anymore, since she is working full time. A victim of her dark moods, yes, but not crazy, only hungering for time to mold her thoughts into expressions. Catharsis?"

"There you go again, a poet in the making. You. Forget about your practice, start writing poetry. Surgeon of the minds, not of the hearts." Gable attempted humor.

"To leave my practice and die in the gutter?" Aslam leaped to his feet. "But you must continue writing, don't waste your talent."

"What talent? Hugging the rags of stupidity and weaving the mantle of mediocrity. God, how I hate myself for wallowing into this mire of stupidity and mediocrity." Gable laughed to drown the cry of hopelessness within him.

"With this pleasant note, I must leave. But I must tell you that your suffering or self-degradation, in medical terminology, is called hebetude." He waved goodbye. "My little ones might go to sleep before I get home, so I better hurry."

"Don't carry the burden of my ignorance with you if you must leave." Gable got to his feet, holding out his hand. "If I understand correctly, hebetude means lethargy, or emotional disinterest, something like that. But don't let me keep you. Can't help asking though, how little are your little ones?"

"Ashan is almost three, and Aiysha is only three weeks old." Aslam sauntered away, followed by Gable.

"How is Heather?" Gable held open the door, breathing in the gloom of the night.

"Bright and beautiful," Aslam said, racing toward his Pinto against the bellows of wind and drizzle.

Twelve ~ Hare-Krishna

Gable sat writing at his desk in his little cubicle of an office in the Publishing House. He was pounding at his typewriter with the fury of a hurricane, the words on the paper jumping and skipping. Bryan was seated at his own desk, cluttered with papers and magazines. He was trying to write, rather stabbing one article with the blows of additions and deletions and getting frustrated. Suddenly, he kicked his chair back and padded toward Gable with an air of urgency. Peering over Gable's shoulders, he stood silent for a moment, and then burst into a litany of complaints.

"This accursed place, how I hate it. It smells of ink, dust and drudgery." Bryan traced the pattern of dust on Gable's desk with his finger.

"How restless you are," Gable commented. "Are you in love, again?"

"Totally and absolutely," Bryan exclaimed. "And this time, it's pure love, nothing sleazy or frivolous, mind you."

"Exquisite and ephemeral, this love of yours." Gable spun his chair around. "It's not in your guts to love someone purely, and absolutely."

"But you have not seen Allison. She even tempts angels to fall in love with her," Bryan sang ecstatically.

"Anything interesting going on?" Gable was unable to share Bryan's enthusiasm, his tone sarcastic.

"What could be more interesting than love?" Bryan assumed an injured expression, trying his best not to smile.

"Caprice for one." Gable smiled back.

"So, you think my love for Allison is just caprice?"

"More so than ever before."

"How do you mean?" Bryan asked.

"You have been singing Allison's praises with such gusto, as if bandaging your will to love before it falls crumbling to pieces," Gable responded.

"And you have lost the will to love, isn't that true?" Bryan teased. "You are afraid of the mere word, *love*, for sure." He planted himself opposite Gable as if geared for a combat.

"Not afraid, just indifferent," Gable replied. "The word *love* is meaningless, as it is," he added defensively.

"Your love for Ethel. Is it love or caprice?"

"Neither. Something sacred and inexpressible. Perhaps, Ethel can find a name for how or what I feel, but I have broken that link, too. And yet, there is a link, the silence which I love."

"Now that Linda has left you, and Fabian and Ethel won't speak with you, what do you plan to do?"

"Nothing, absolutely nothing," Gable responded. "Neither the will to live, nor the courage to die, does this sound familiar?"

"Yes. And what a pity. You would be buried alive into the great tomb of this world with all its reek of banality and selfishness." Bryan got to his feet. "Life is both a dream and a nightmare, inside the vacuum of *ego*, compelling us to fill this vacuum with tears or laughter, a sort of commandment to fight death with the breath of labor and creativity, until the vacuum itself chokes us to nothingness, or to the eternal curse in living." He waved his arms hopelessly. "You have grown so morbid. I know what you need, new friends, and new experiences. Drop by this evening at my place. You must meet Lisa. She is a disciple of Hare-Krishna, a fascinating character. She is expert on meditation and quite a fanatic, stressing her viewpoint that mediation is the panacea for all ills, including grief and suffering."

"Sure," Gable declared. "A few mantras toward the road to oblivion would make us all the insufferable dolts, if we already are not *that*." Gable laughed.

"Good. That means, you would come." Bryan waved happily. He scurried back to his desk; his laughter filling the office in rivulets of sunshine.

Gable had worked late at the office, poring over dull articles and editing the lengthy manuscripts. The evening had descended quickly, his promise to Bryan to join him crushing him down with the weight of steel in indecision. He had tried to rest in his room with his head cradled in his hands, but ending up pacing. The rain was beating against the windows of his bedroom, and the sky was growing dark, much like his thoughts on the rungs of chaos and revolt. Finally, he had decided in favor of his promise to Bryan, tossing his tie on the bed and scribbling a couple of lines to his villanelle before fleeing his room.

Sorrows weep no more, aged grief has turned all gray
Negation in nothingness dares to flee
All thoughts are dunes of sand and mind a pot of clay

Gable was oblivious to the dark, wet evening, only the words of his villanelle whistling in his head, as he drove toward Bryan's house. The violence of nature in torrents of rain and billowing clouds seemed not to penetrate his thoughts as he kept drifting into the dream-world of traffic under the dictates of caution and discipline. The hurricanes of chaos and confusion inside him had abated, his thoughts donning the mantle of apathy and inertia. The mists of silence had enveloped him so completely that he had no idea how and when he had reached Bryan's apartment. Only when he lit a cigarette while sunk deep into the wicker chair did he become aware of the chill of loneliness within him and of the shadow of timelessness. Bryan was pouring whiskey and soda in two glasses against the dimly-lit corner of this living-room, his back toward Gable, and Gable had this strange feeling of being an intruder even within the cold chambers of his own thoughts.

Gable had never visited Bryan's apartment before, but as he sat puffing on his cigarette, an eerie feeling crept up into his thoughts that he had been here before in the company of someone else inside some remote bubble of time. The wall-to-wall bookshelves with musty odor were whispering to him of another life long forgotten. The small lamps with dark shades over the escritoire and the bust of Socrates were so familiar and palpitating, as if slicing the silence within him with the knives of memories past, or of future hallucinations. So absorbed was he in this strange, amorphous world of his past living that he didn't notice Bryan holding out the glass of drink to him.

"Are you finding the clutter and the dull furnishings to your liking?" Bryan asked, forcing the glass into Gable's hand.

"Splendid," Gable said, jolted out of his reveries.

Before Bryan could comment, the door bell chimed, and he lunged toward the door, admitting Lisa ceremoniously.

"Terrible night, isn't it?" Bryan said and then sang his introduction with one sweeping curtsy of his arm. "The wet star of the evening, lovely Lisa." He stood laughing, watching Gable stumble to his feet as if dazed.

"Pleasure meeting you." Gable could barely talk, gazing into the large, hazel pools of her eyes.

"Gable is my friend. Unfortunately, dull and untalented. Though claiming, rather striving, to become the author of a bestseller." Bryan turned to pour another drink.

"So gracious of him to hold me in such high esteem, don't you think?" Gable smiled, still gazing into her eyes.

"He is gracious only to himself, as far as I can judge." Lisa smiled back, lowering herself into the settee opposite Gable.

Bryan returned with the drink and soon the conversation drifted beyond jokes and laughter into the realm of health and meditation. Gable had become a silent participant, listening with a rapt attention as if caught into the vortex of a dream. Everything within his sight were either blown out of proportion, or reduced to insignificance. The lamps were burning brighter; the books were fading into parchments, all dry and shriveled. Bryan's face was haloed by pale mists, and Lisa's eyes were bright as the stars. He himself was the ghost of the night, half drunk, half listening, and utterly smitten by the charming face and voice of Lisa.

"Peace of Mind is not a commodity to be bartered into the open market of greed and selfishness." Lisa was goaded by Bryan to expound. "Paradoxically, peace of mind has nothing to do with mind, but with heart. A pure heart scraped clean of all pride. A heart, wearing the shield of faith and love. Everyone has to fashion that shield according to one's own need and desire. My shield is Hare-Krishna, offering me peace and consolation. Hope and love and the promise of unity with all, to be precise. You should come with me to the Temple of Gold in Virginia and discover for yourself the nuggets of peace and love." The tremor of reverence in her voice was reflected in her eyes.

"Hare-Krishna, the wounded limb of Hinduism, isn't that it?" Bryan's eyes were lit up with mischief. "Witchcraft, not peace and love. Those lunatics at the Temple of Gold have hypnotized you, demanding absolute obedience to their absolute wills and neglecting to observe that you've become a rebel, defying the wishes of your parents. You yourself told me that your parents forbid you to associate with them, but you don't give a hoot, do you?"

"The choice is simple any fool can figure that out," Lisa sang ecstatically. "In order to obey my conscience, I have to disobey my parents. Follow my bliss, sort of. Or, peace of mind, which my parents think is unattainable. It's all illusion, they say, and they think they are the masters of their own fates. Not knowing that fates are our masters, and we their slaves. I'm merely obeying the laws of nature, in search of peace, seeking further to embrace all into this fold of peace and unity."

"You have a most willing candidate here, then." Bryan's laughter was seeking the attention of his reticent friend. "In quest of peace and unity, Gable would not only dare enter a temple, but wade through the fires of hell if genuinely convinced."

"No such quest is needed since I know the abode of peace and unity." Gable breathed enigmatically. "I'm no stranger to the fires of hell, and the tortures of the damned I have suffered already, but to dwell on that would present a very dull argument." He shifted his gaze to Lisa. "It would be my sole delight and privilege to visit the temple, Lisa, though for reasons quite contrary as presumed by Bryan."

"The reasons, whatever they may be, are superfluous. The important thing is that you would come to the temple." Lisa fished out a card from her purse, a subtle flush creeping over her cheeks. "Looking forward to your visit." She sprang to her feet, slipping the card into Gable's hand. "Must run before my parents lock me out." She bid hasty goodbyes and rushed out before Bryan could get to his feet.

"So, Lisa has hypnotized you." Bryan flung this comment over his shoulders as he marched away to get more drinks.

"Her eyes are beautiful, changing from gray to opalescent like the loveliest of dawns," Gable replied.

"You are positively drunk." Bryan held out the glass of whiskey and soda to Gable. "We would drink 'til we fall senseless."

"For you to reach to that state, you need a barrel of whiskey." Gable laughed, lighting a cigarette.

"How very true, but you are hopeless." Bryan chuckled, sinking into his chair.

"Hopeless, a meaningless word just like the word love," Gable responded.

"You are right." Bryan was feeling relaxed and lightheaded. "Such fools we are, always trying to find meaning in love."

"Why do I have this feeling that when you agree with me, you're pulling my leg?" Never mind, platitudes don't amuse me anymore. Though raw, naked reality gnaws within me like some foul canker. How abominably I behaved, not only hurting Ethel, but destroying the bond of friendship with Fabian. They both despise me, I'm sure. Is forgiveness possible?" His heart was drugged with pain, and his thoughts muddled.

"Your madness would be forgotten, and you would be forgiven, I predict." Bryan prophesied with a grin.

"I don't want to be forgiven, and would be happy if punished."

"Self-pity. You are the victim of self-pity, Gable. And it would drown you deeper into the mire of your own pain and confusion." Bryan laughed.

"A sort of blessing when one can feel comfortable wallowing into the mire of one's pain and gloat over one's own sense of degradation?" Gable quipped. "This foul pit of torment inside me is deep enough for my mighty sins." His lips widened into an Epicurean smile.

"Such noble sins," Bryan declared

. "Believe it or not, I am sinless, and I am good. Goodness is me," he chanted.

"Empirical goodness?" Gable pounced with the spirit of an Athenian warlord. "Do you believe in God?"

"Only in goodness," Bryan muttered.

"God might forgive you for such levity." Gable could not hold still the wheel of his thoughts. "At least you won't blame God for all the misfortunes in this world."

"Who is to blame whom?" Bryan's thoughts were gathering fogs in memories.

"Now, you are positively drunk, no doubt," Gable commented, as if confirming his own state of intoxication. "You better go to bed before I have to carry you there."

"You are the fine one to tell me that, as if you are sober yourself." Bryan winked and giggled. "Isn't it noble to get drunk, it opens doors to the profoundest of mysteries concealed within oneself, lending voice to one's psyche and offering solutions to problems. A barrage of questions which need answers. What are our interests? Which of our actions afford us pleasures? What is happiness? Is sorrow real? Why are we here and what is our quest in life?"

"We are here to follow the mists of happiness, ethereal and illusive. That is our quest. To long for something unattainable and to suffer in return with joy and gloating."

"Fools that we are. Why don't we despise the very word happiness, and attain what is within the realm of our puny intelligence? Love, peace and surrender."

"Fools, indeed. For suffering is our *need*. We truly live when we suffer." Gable yawned. "Without the feast of suffering, how can one ever taste the fruits of love, hope?"

"Our shadows are more real than our bodies. Neither feasting on suffering, nor hungering for the crumbs of happiness. A lesson to learn if we can only pause and witness their peace and silence," Bryan uttered.

"A shadow can't contain the light of love, yet body is love, radiating light and lending form to the shadow." Gable could hear the whistle of snoring from Bryan's open mouth, his own lips and eyes closing.

Gable's head lolled to one side as he tried to catch the string of his thoughts, but the string was slippery and wagging its tail in some mad dance of frenzy and defiance. He might have dozed off, for when he opened his eyes, he could see Bryan sprawled on the floor, snoring away. Gable tried to get up, the strip of carpet between him and the front door rising like a swinging bridge which he dared not cross. Summoning courage, he eased himself up laboriously, then stood maintaining his balance. For a few moments he watched Bryan, but to him an eternity elapsed before he shut the door behind him and stumbled out on the front porch.

Blessed is the breath which knows not that it breathes. Gable's face was stung by the whiff of cold air, and he couldn't take another step.

The sky had cleared, and the moonlit night with all its glory of starry brilliance was holding Gable captive, but his legs were trembling, and he found himself slouching down to the bare floor, his hands clutching the white balustrade. His gaze was fixed to the livid moon, the silvery and luminescent sky sending chills down his spine, his body shivering. A blade of ice had cut through his heart, and he thought he was dying. Fortunately, he was drifted into the comfort of sleep, though dreams were awakening with all their fury of thunder and lightning.

Beloved, Beloved. The bolts of light and chaos in Gable's dreams were pleading to be near Ethel.

One cry of agony in Gable's heart was caught inside the abyss of the night. He was imprisoned inside the jungle of his own dreams, much like a wounded prisoner, alone and disconsolate. Dark and desolate dreams were merging and yet he slept chilled inside the blankets of cold and silence. He must have slept long and deep, for when he opened his eyes, his gaze fell on the Cardinal perched on the bush nearby like a red jewel from the very bowl of dawn.

Gable was lumbering to his feet, stiff and aching, now intoxicated by the beauty of the dusk. His very soul was shuddering, filled with awe, as if he was witnessing a holy miracle, etched alive in timelessness. He could see the crimson wound inside his heart, all beautiful and healed. Suddenly, it was aching again, reaching out to the reflection of gold and glory in sunshine with a longing of surrender.

Thirteen ~ Davie in Love

Gable was feeling a strange sense of peace while seated in the comfort of his own bedroom. He was eating lunch, goaded by his mother, who sat opposite him to make sure that he finished everything on his plate. Last night's drunkenness had left him despondent as well as exhilarated, but this afternoon he was sober and rather sullen. Wrapped in his blue bathrobe, with a red blanket over his knees, he looked like the emblem of American peace and prosperity. There were blue circles under his eyes, and his pallor was enhanced by the flash of gold in his hair swept back from his brow. He was sipping his coffee. His mother was smiling, quite satisfied that he had cleaned his plate under her strict vigilance and with utmost obedience.

"Hot bath and good food, isn't it a blessing, Gable?" Mrs. Faulkner commented. "What sense is there to drown your body in gallons of whiskey and then let it suffer cold and neglect?" She continued with a dint of reproof. "You are suffering, I know. But don't you know that when you suffer your mother suffers too? Each little hurt that you feel I feel too." She stopped, noticing the flash of remorse in Gable's eyes.

"I know, Mom, and that causes me double the pain and grief, believe me," Gable admitted. "I didn't intend to get drunk. I try not to do anything which would hurt you, and I end up doing just the same. But I will try harder, Mom, I promise, I will. Forgive me."

"You have my forgiveness, son, but I am not sure about your dad." Mrs. Faulkner heaved herself up. "Some sort of punishment is in store for you, I can tell." She gathered the empty cup and plate in the tray and stood smiling. "You have rested enough, now get some writing done, and mold your talent toward something noble and constructive." She scurried out without saying another word.

Gable sat numb and unmoving, staring at his red blanket as if the blood from his very heart had congealed in this fabric of warmth and comfort. He closed his eyes, the sting of memories was sharp and cutting. His thoughts were billowing forth, tearing down the veil of silence. How long did he sit there molded in the blanket of inertia, he had no recollection, only the awareness of one whirlwind of a thought.

Recognize this great curse, *you are destined to hurt the women you love the most. Mom, Maryana, Beloved—* this whirlwind of a thought was swept asunder by the tinkling of his mother's voice.

Mrs. Faulkner was standing by the door, Fabian at her elbow, while Gable blinked away this vision of incredulity. Mrs. Faulkner was leaving, her voice amorphous inside the icy depths of Gable's awareness.

"Someone here to see you, Gable." Gable could hear the echo of his mother's voice piercing his heart, his gaze fixed to Fabian. "Fabian." One tremor of a greeting escaped his lips. It was rather a cry of despair, kneeling at the hearth of fate.

"I had the impression you were frightfully ill." Fabian marched right into the room. "Don't stand on ceremony, I'll make myself comfortable." His eyes were lit by the lamps of sarcasm, as he lowered himself into a chair beside his friend.

"Fabian." Gable murmured again. "You have forgiven me. How could you forgive a fool like me?" He averted his gaze.

"*To err is human.* Who said that, Alexander Pope or Shakespeare, who cares?" Fabian said nonchalantly.

"Is it true you have really forgiven me?" Gable asked, disbelief mirrored in his eyes as blue icicles.

"I'm experimenting on this theory, if forgiveness is divine." Fabian laughed. "In reality, if there is any credence to this word as something *real*, I have come here to talk about the noble madness of us three. You, me, and Maryana's. Your madness is love and suffering. Mine, some nameless affliction to know God and forgiveness. Maryana's, a rare incurable disease, nourished by the sense of self-alienation and self-immolation." He paused, his look sad and distant. "The more I thought about your particular madness, the more I understood it, I think. You didn't mean to offend me, or Ethel, for that matter. Follies are not insults, though they both rise to the heights of absurdity when goaded by madness. Yes, we are the victims of our madness. You, me, Maryana." He seemed to be lost into his own well of silent contemplations.

"Maryana." Gable could barely murmur, as if tasting the salt of pain on his lips. "You were in love with Maryana, were you not? Why didn't you marry her?"

"No pious jury is going to convict me of such holiness," Fabian replied evasively. "I thought we were talking about forgiveness." He laughed rather nervously.

"Madness. As I recall. We were talking about madness." Gable's eyes were lit with a sudden challenge, compelling his friend to confess.

"Another act of madness if I'm goaded into revealing the secrets of my heart." Fabian said defensively.

"When madness befriends madness, no ripples of secrets remain unexplored."

"Then madness speaks, not me. Yet, it is me." Fabian said. "I loved her, but couldn't marry her. She loved you more than she loved me."

A rock of silence hit both friends as they sat gazing into each other's eyes for more answers. Fabian's look was sad. Bewilderment was shining in Gable's eyes. In his mind's vision was the white nymph of youth and beauty, his sister. Adoring and worshipping him. The bubbles of grief were bursting inside him, and his thoughts were knocking at the gates of oblivion. Fabian was the first one to break away from this spell of silence by the gentle ripple of a song from Ethel's lips. Ethel had stolen into the room unnoticed.

"These bullets of silence look so very dangerous," Ethel chimed while drifting toward the statues of silence.

"Ethel." Fabian leaped to his feet.

"Ethel," Gable said. "Forgive me," he pleaded.

"What's in the past is forgotten and forgiven, Gable. Let's not mention it, please." Ethel smiled, turning her attention to Fabian. "Sorry to impose on this confidential meeting, but we must leave. Kimberly must be getting impatient ...." She paused, becoming aware of Fabian's puzzled expression. "Don't tell me you forgot? We promised our daughter a ride in the park."

"How could I forget when I am looking forward to it?" Fabian glossed his forgetfulness with a broad smile. "Friends." He held out his hands, which Gable grasped with warmth of gratitude.

"Friends," Gable replied.

"Goodbye," Ethel chanted merrily. "You owe us a visit ... soon." She grabbed Fabian's arm and dragged him toward the door.

Gable stood still; his farewell barely audible. He could hear the footsteps fading down the staircase, but he was a statue of ice, unable to move or think. The ice and chill inside him were breaking, and he was stumbling toward the staircase as if drunk. Some subtle sting of loneliness was crawling inside his heart like a serpent, and he was sinking into the cushioned seat in the foyer, oblivious to his pain and surroundings. Some sort of white abyss within him was tearing its veil of silence, and in its radiance were etched *two faces, those of Ethel and Maryana.* The resemblance was so stark as if they were one face with two names, staring back at him through the mists of love.

Trembling inwardly, Gable closed his eyes, the lips of his soul kissing some altar of peace. An astonishing sense of comfort was closing around him, unlocking the casket of *hope* and *destiny*. He was going to live, truly live inside the paradise of hope where destiny had decreed that he would be near Ethel, always. That there could never be any gulf or separation from his beloved

Ethel, my sight and my soul. Gable's thoughts were kindling the fire of madness. *How am I supposed to live? As all men do? Nurturing hope and wallowing into the offal of their lusts and desires?* His thoughts were snipped short by the sharp declaration of Davie, who had wheeled his chair into the foyer noiselessly.

"Blessed are the wise and the indolent." Davie's epigram was biting into Gable's awareness, his eyes shot open.

"And cursed are the ones who love truly," Gable responded.

"Love is an experience and a blessing as I view it." Davie laughed. "But the word *love* is meaningless as it is being used these days. Fit to be pressed inside the pages of a book with all its reek of lies and banality. You are the writer, Gable. Rename *love* and mold it into something profound and palpitating. Make it a religion, if you will."

"The pious artist in you, Davie, how I have failed to notice." Gable sighed to himself. "How can I write when the horror of prison still haunts me, when Ethel's marriage holds a knife to my heart, and when my own reckless will stands like a rock of shame over my shoulders?"

His look was distant, rather enigmatic. "Did you ever feel that Maryana loved me the most?"

"She worshipped you," Davie responded, a bit puzzled by the question. "Mom loves me the most; dad loves Maryana the best, so love in our family is equally distributed," he added quickly, noticing the troubled look in his brother's eyes. "Where is Aslam, I haven't seen him since months?"

"Your thoughts are as disjointed as mine," Gable said thoughtfully. "Aslam has whisked away his family to Pakistan for a visit. Invited me, too, even offered to buy my ticket, but I declined. Should have gone. But then I was hoping you'd get married. Do you think your engagement is a big secret?"

"Not really. I told Mom, and she can't hold a secret." Davie smiled. "Let me quiz you, Gable. Which passion is worthy of fulfillment, falling in love, or forgetting the same love?"

"Strange that you quiz your brother on something trite like love. To fall in love is as easy as breathing and to forget the same love as difficult as holding one's breath until eternity. So, judge for yourself."

"What a glorious explosion it would be, when that breath is released," Davie teased.

"I envy the purity of your heart, Davie. You are wedded to your music, and you'll not ever suffer."

"In other words, I am heartless," Davie replied.

"On the contrary, you have a very loving heart." Gable forced his gaze to rest on Davie with the intensity of a philosopher. "Yes, your passionate heart, I fear the most, to be easily deceived by the charms of beauty. Well, I hope, you don't love Phoebe more than your music. Music soothes and liberates. Love, it injures and annihilates."

"Does love ever pour joy into one's heart, Gable?" Davie asked.

"Unpredictable as it is, it does pour joy, abundantly at times. And rarely, most of the time," Gable said. "Love's hunger for pain is enormous and its appetite for joy very little, unless one learns how to starve its hungers and expand its appetites."

"Little of both are enough to make me content, if not happy," Davie replied.

"You are fortunate," Gable exclaimed. "If I could love less, I would learn to live the most."

"Could anyone make you forget Ethel?" Davie asked.

"That unforgettable sweetness? No." Gable jumped to his feet and plodded away, burdened by the weight of his own despair.

Fourteen ~ Madness Supreme

Spirit of agony has lost its power to slay
The embittered heart in torments of glee
All thoughts are dunes of sand and mind a pot of clay

These fresh lines of his villanelle were juggling in Gable's head as he sat in his office. He was punching the characters of his own novel with bold strokes and not even aware that he had scribbled these three lines on a separate piece of paper and had pushed it aside. He continued to merge feverishly with the spilling of words on the stack of papers before him. Bryan was seated at his own desk, stabbing the articles with the fury of his caprice and restlessness. Unable to concentrate, he sprang to his feet and tiptoed to Gable's desk. Gable sat oblivious to his friend's presence behind him. Bryan's eyes caught the lines of the villanelle and he burst out laughing.

"If your thoughts are as costive as your expressions, you better abandon this trade of writing." Bryan stood, singing the lines of villanelle to himself.

"Insufferable fool, that's what you are." Gable stopped writing. "You have stumped the brains of my protagonist with the fire of your intrusion."

"Those dull, cellophane characters in your novel. You're wasting your time," Bryan quipped. "Besides, it's time to eat and I am starving. That sleazy bar down the street, their hamburgers are delicious and their prices deliciously low. Want to join me?"

"If gluttony doesn't kill you, cheap burgers will." Gable swung his chair around to face the laughing bully.

"That means you're coming, to witness my death." Bryan strode toward the door, Gable following.

The cold sunshine with stinging brightness was a breathtaking experience from the damp, cheerless office. But Gable was oblivious to this golden day as he stood on the sidewalk waiting for the green signal. Bryan next to him was shielding his eyes and grumbling inanities.

"Holy cow, this sunshine is making me blind," Bryan declared while stalking ahead of Gable to reach the sleazy bar.

"You're not worthy of such affliction as blindness which, in fact, is a blessing."

"Your mad epigrams are making my stomach churn." Bryan raced toward the dilapidated building, scraped open the door and stormed into the dingy room.

This sunless, crowded bar was a balmy relief to Bryan. Gable made himself comfortable at the greasy table, shuddering inwardly. He ordered a bowl of clam-chowder, watching it suspiciously before taking a spoonful. Bryan was enjoying his hamburger and French fries, his gaze following the voluptuous waitress as he took a large gulp of beer.

"How smooth and refreshing." Bryan breathed, relishing the taste of his drink.

"Could it be the beer or the waitress?" Gable asked.

"Beer, of course." Bryan laughed, returning his gaze to Gable. "She wouldn't be smooth, I assure you."

"Refreshing, perhaps, since you couldn't help devouring, while relishing your luncheon." Gable elicited a chuckle.

"It would be truly refreshing if you could explain your blind comment as to blindness being a blessing," Bryan said.

"This skyrocketing bill is beyond my budget." Gable attempted to study the bill with an air of amusement.

"What a parsimonious lout. You look ridiculous when you try to be evasive. Lunch is on me."

"That sounds fair." Gable pushed the bill toward Bryan and lit a cigarette. "Being ridiculous is in vogue. Or, it has been thus since the time of creation. If we could look deep within us, we would discover that we are nothing but fools."

"Why not stay happy and ignorant?" Bryan inquired.

"Inside the marshland of our own ignorance, we think we are the masters of our fates," Gable commented.

"My fault entirely, to introduce you to Lisa. I can hear her speaking through you." Bryan arched his eyebrows, replenishing his glass of beer from the jug. "You are out of your wits lately, and you have met her only twice. I have this feeling that you're losing your mind, in some sort of demented way, metaphorically."

"A noble dementia, literally," Gable confessed. "Wearied of my pain and passion, I'm searching for peace. And Lisa is the perfect guide to lead me toward it, hopefully."

"Peace in the cult of Hare-Krishna, absolutely not." Bryan echoed his inner disdain. "You won't find peace anywhere but within you, and you know it."

"Inside the ocean of my agony there is no room for peace." Gable laughed.

"Singing mantras in the dark or dancing barefoot in the temple is not going to melt your agony." Bryan waved his arm sanctimoniously. "You might be cloaked in the saffron robe of absurdity, but you won't find peace."

"It's unchristian to fly into rage, don't you know?" Gable mocked.

"As one Christian to another then, I advise that you stay away from this cult of Hare-Krishna. Some dark power is pulling you toward the dungeon of illusion and ignorance."

"What zeal. Do I have the privilege to presume that you are trying to save me from the fires of perdition?" Gable asked. "Carving a path toward salvation for me, how ridiculous."

"You have no soul, Gable," Bryan declared.

"Then why bother preaching?"

"Because I am a bigger fool than you. Hoping to lead you by the tail of spirituality whose head of wisdom is cut off," Bryan replied.

"I agree." Gable got to his feet.

"So, you won't go barefooted dancing on the streets?" Bryan chuckled, snatching his wallet out at the sight of the waitress.

"I agreed only of *you* being the bigger fool ...." Gable could not continue, trailing away to escape his own madness.

Fifteen ~ Temple of Gold

The Temple of Gold was in a golden haze in the background as Gable promenaded past the lotus pond with Lisa. He was quiet, draped in saffron robe, his shaved head a shining globe. He was contemplating the past six months of his self-exile into this kingdom of magic and mystery. A panorama of lakes and colonnades with marble gods and goddess', all garlanded, were beckoning him to stay, as if cognizant of his decision to leave this very afternoon.

The knowing self is not born, it does not, it sprang from nothing; nothing sprang from it. The firm holding back of the senses is called yoga. Gable's mind was chanting these words expressed by his guru, Shiriji. *I really admire a fellow who goes about the whole day with a well-fed stomach and a vacuous mind.* This aphorism of Confucius was now hitting him on the head.

Gable was becoming aware of Lisa beside him, wrapped in white sari and calm as the mirrored lakes, but he dared not utter a word lest he break the spell of tranquility within and without. His was looking to the emerald hills in the distance. All were mists and illusions above and beyond. His sight was returning to the earthly paradise where bowers of roses were spilling perfumes and geraniums in brass pots. His attention was diverted to the children, riding their bikes like the wind and chortling with glee. This scene of joy and purity was teasing the strings of his thoughts that were discordant tunes in stark contrast to the dreamy landscape.

As leaves on trees, such is the life of man. Gable's mind was scraping away this line of homer as if digging through the boundaries of time. *Who am I? Where am I? What do I seek?* He could hear the quiet woe of his solitary contemplations. *No temple could heal my soul, no church to dispel my agony, no religion to cure my hopelessness.* His ears were drinking the nectar of hymns.

Hare-Rama, Hare-Krishna, these chants from the lips of the devotees were floating in the air and merging with the sunshine. These sounds were one voice, one melody from the ladies in white saris who were tending the garden as if drunk with the wine. *OM, OM,* this great sound was rippling aloft from the little temple across the lake and billowing as the hymn of holiness.

"The mystical throb of joy in these mantras, mingling with the sadness of the whole world," Gable said, not looking at Lisa.

"The hymns of the gods themselves, spraying the power of wisdom, if one were to listen closely," Lisa replied, quick to notice the presence of the Guru Shiriji amongst the saffron-robed disciples.

"Yes, the logic and the wisdom—"

Gable could not continue, becoming aware of the guru's approach, leaving his disciples behind.

"Have you found nirvana, Gable?" Shiriji's voice melted in the air like a caress.

"Nirvana?" Gable considered the smiling eyes of the Guru.

"Yes, nirvana." Shiriji appeared to taste the word before he continued. "Nirvana is where the manifestation of Noble Wisdom expresses itself in Perfect Love for all. It is where the manifestation of Perfect Love expresses itself in Noble Wisdom for enlightenment of all—there indeed is Nirvana. You found it once, but lost it. You are going to leave us, this very afternoon, possibly?"

"You have read my mind, Guruji," Gable murmured humbly. "Can you look into my soul, too?"

"Into the mind and soul of nature even. Stars of fate are my favorite to hold and behold, their reflections engraved inside the souls of the human beings." His compassion was reaching out to Gable.

"What does my star of fate reveal?" Gable asked.

"Much more than I can reveal," Shiriji began thoughtfully. "Two furrows I see in there. One holding the ruby wounds of love for one girl alone. And the other gouged by the longing to write. A mound of bliss is waiting there at the end, linked to one tortuous channel, through which success and fulfillment are bound to ripple. Yes, your star of fate is shining with the promise of love and achievement. In between sufferings are great, but then rewards bountiful."

"Mockery of fate, I can hear it." The taut ridges around Gable's lips were relaxing.

"Tongues of destiny have no sounds, no expressions, only impressions," Shiriji said. "You have accomplished much here and now you must move on. The world is waiting to embrace you into its gluttonous arms. Come, walk up to my hermitage, this last time, perhaps." He resumed his walk, Gable following. "Time has allowed you to finish your novel and that was one of your duties inside the maze of this world."

"You never fail to amaze me, Guruji. How did you know I finished my novel? Did you read that in my stars? I don't understand."

"Don't try to understand everything lest you become ignorant of everything," Shiriji quoted, his pace accelerating at each step.

"Democritus," Gable thought aloud.

"So, you are well versed in philosophy as well as in theology?"

"In theophanies and theogonies, too, not to mention the bibulous cults of the Aborigines."

"This Temple of Gold, Guruji, so mysterious, so enchanting." The spirit of sadness in Gable was uttering these words. "What's the secret of its mystery and enchantment?"

"My son, this is God's house much like any other church, mosque or synagogue." Shiriji began gently. "In fact, this entire world is the holy temple of God. The only difference between other places of worship and this is that people go there to pray, and they come here to seek, to surrender and to lose oneself in the oneness of God. They come here burdened with the need for oblivion, which is striving toward bliss supreme and wisdom sublime. This need is more savage than the need for food, shelter or survival. Some try to satisfy this need with drugs, or alcohol, or even working tirelessly, but attaining neither bliss, nor wisdom, only endless suffering. Here, we drink only love. The cup of unconditional love, not tainted by the froth of hell, horror or retribution. Love, not fear, is the essence of this place called holiness. If you have felt the former and abandoned the latter, you have found the link to God and humanity." He paused before entering his hermitage. "Won't you share a cup of honeyed tea with me before you leave?" He stood smiling under the birch tree, his eyes spilling warmth.

"My delight entirely," Gable uttered reverently.

***

Another day, another time, yet pain was lingering like a shadow. Gable, seated at the desk in his bedroom could feel the sting of memories where the Temple of Gold stood like a dream. He had returned home only a week ago, but had been writing feverishly since then, neglecting his family and friends. Though writing most devotedly, his neglected villanelle was teasing his memory, so he grabbed that piece of paper and scribbled more lines.

Surcease has trodden all paths to pave the way
Into the chambers of hope where blindness can see
All thoughts are dunes of sand and mind a pot of clay

Gable kept looking at the lines, pen poised in his hand, his mind jogging back to the hermitage where Guru Shiriji had pounded the essence of all religions into one commandment.

Brahmanism: *This is the sum of duty: Do not unto others which would cause you pain if done unto you.*

Buddhism: *Hurt not others in ways that you yourself would find hurtful.*

The pen was slipping from Gable's hands, he could neither think, nor write. The familiar ache of love and longing was an open wound in his heart, repeating the beloved name, Ethel, Ethel. He leaped to his feet, looking out of the window, his very soul pleading for the nearness of beloved. But he stood there awed and humbled. The sunset had arrested him, its own heart a portrait of sorrow, purple wounds of agony in vermilion.

Sixteen ~ Mundane World

The square living-room at Fabian's home with beige sofas and Queen Ann furniture was offering Gable a rare delight and comfort. Kimberly was snuggling closer to Ethel as if afraid of this stranger called Uncle Gable, with shaven head and luminous eyes. Fabian was oblivious to any change in his friend's manner or appearance, joking and laughing good-heatedly.

"Never thought you would escape that gilded prison of a Temple of Gold, in my lifetime." Fabian laughed in response to Gable's panegyric account of that holy retreat.

"It was difficult, but had to come to this mundane world of family and friends," Gable quipped, shifting his attention to Ethel. "Couldn't stay away from Kimberly. She has forgotten me already and is afraid." He flashed a warm look at the cowering child.

"Yes, she is a little afraid. Doesn't recognize you with your head shaved," Ethel said sweetly. "A thatch of hair on your head and she would come running to you." She hugged her daughter. "He is your uncle Gable, remember."

"The same foolish uncle, my dear, who threw you up in the air and caught you into his arms," Gable boasted, encouraged by the diffident smile of Kimberly.

"A foolish friend, I must add, who has neglected us all most besottedly." Fabian sought Gable's attention. "What mystery is there in this cult of Hare-Krishna? What charm, what wisdom, if any?"

"As much charm and wisdom as in the parables of all world religions, which are imitating still the rites of the pagans in devotion to their gods immortal. And as for the mystery, one needs many lives to explore its depths."

"Infidel you were and infidel you would remain," Fabian chanted hilariously. "But I am glad you have left the unexplored depths and would be visiting us often."

"Often enough for you to beg me to stay away." Gable replied. "I have to come to hug and spoil Kimberly." He flashed another warm glance at her. "Would you talk to me, Kimberly, if I came often?"

"Yees." Kimberly's flowerlike face was wreathed in a smile. "Why don't you have hair?" She giggled.

"Kimberly," Ethel admonished. "Forgive her for her lack of manners, Gable, she doesn't understand."

"Children should be rewarded for their honesty. We are the ones who need to be forgiven. For our follies, I am sure." Gable's expression was tender. "With a comical head like mine, most children would be curious, if not frightened." He fixed his gaze to Kimberly. "Come, my dear, we will be friends." He held out his arms.

"I'm not afraid." Kimberly skipped and bounced right into Gable's arms.

"Sing to Uncle Gable that song grandma taught you," Ethel coaxed as her daughter settled into Gable's lap.

"Yes, yes, we want to hear it," Gable and Fabian urged in unison.

"Mary had a wittle wamb, Mary had a wittle wamb, Mary had a wittle wamb." Kimberly was repeating the same line, trying her best to remember the other.

"Your needle is stuck, honey." Ethel could not control her laughter amidst the chiming of the door-bell.

Fabian got to his feet and scrambled to the front door. Gable was laughing, stealing a look at Ethel, his heart awakening with a pang of love. Fabian soon returned, Bryan following at his heels. Kimberly had abandoned Gable's lap, prancing and giggling, but noticing Bryan she stood still, her expression puzzled.

"Is that my uncle, too?" Kimberly asked innocently.

"I am your real uncle." Bryan planted a little kiss on her forehead.

"Would the real uncle care for a cup of coffee?" Ethel eased herself up, her look voicing the same question to Gable and Fabian.

After hearing the eager chant of all three friends, Ethel glided away to fetch coffee, Kimberly racing after her. An awkward silence ensued before Bryan grunted an inquiry.

"What brings you here?" Bryan asked.

"Am I entitled to ask you the same question?" Gable bristled back.

"After you satisfy me with your prudent response." Bryan grinned.

"Prudence never dictates my thoughts, I'm only the slave of my impulses. After I abandoned the sanctuary of bliss, I was anxious to renew my contact with friends. Missed my parents, not knowing that a pleasant surprise awaited me upon my return."

"In other words, you've abandoned Lisa. Left her in the sanctuary of bliss, alone?" Bryan asked heedlessly.

"What surprise?" Fabian tossed his own missile of query.

"Who do I answer first? To the hooligan of jealousy, or to the demon of curiosity?" Gable's gaze swept from one to the other with a sparkling intensity. "Demon wins. Davie, engaged for the longest time, is finally getting married. This goodly surprise itself has banished me from the dungeon of my seclusion."

"Davie? In love?" A cry of joy and amazement escaped Fabian's lips. "He will be joining the crowd."

"What's so good about joining the crowd?" Bryan scoffed.

"What is it this time, Bryan? What infernal madness? You look positively drugged. With what, I don't know?" Gable's tone was rather gentle.

"I'm roasting alive inside the fires of love and despair," Bryan declared with a sigh of relief. "This girl, she even follows me in my dreams like a hideous nightmare. Upon awakening, I feel drenched with shame and guilt, fear clutching me with pincers of torture and hopelessness."

"A lout like you, how could you feel all that?" Fabian asked.

"I am knee-deep in trouble, Gable." Bryan dismissed Fabian and clung to Gable's sympathy alone. "The girl I am talking about is pregnant and insists on marriage. I'm not ready for that commitment, though I loathe myself for not being responsible for my own actions. No more love for me, all my romantic notions are chucked into the fire of confusion. I want to die. Or join Hare-Krishna, Temple of Gold, my sanctuary."

"A sanctuary for us all morons!" Gable laughed. He was about to offer his advice or sympathy when Ethel drifted back into the room.

"For all the morons, only one cup of coffee each." Ethel held out one mug from her tray for Fabian. "The first one for my husband."

"Your husband is no moron, my dear, only his friends are." Fabian claimed the mug, feigning an injured expression. "Can you believe Davie is getting married? Gable the moron himself told us."

"Davie?" Ethel turned quickly, holding out the next mug to Gable. "How wonderful. Who's the lucky girl?"

"Phoebe," Gable said, his heart lurching at the nearness of his own beloved. "He composes symphonies in her praise. A poet's dream with dream-boat eyes, he sings."

"So very romantic." Ethel snatched more mugs from her tray. She handed one mug to Bryan, keeping the last one for herself.

"Dream-girls with dream-boats eyes are demons in disguise, Gable." Bryan said with a feverish intensity. "You better stay out of harm's way, get yourself an apartment. That's my advice for your own benefit. Demons are quick to plant the seeds of evil in men's hearts."

"No room left in my heart for more evils." Gable elicited one mock lament, his heart aching and sinking for some nameless reason.

"Since pre-historic times, demonic traits are ascribed to men alone," Ethel declared in defiance, lowering herself beside her husband.

"You are wicked, Bryan, absolutely wicked," Gable said, his heart thundering to absorb Ethel into its own pain and loneliness.

"About my wickedness, you already know, what have you learned from the Sanctuary of Gold?" Bryan asked.

"Nothing but patience and dullness." Gable smiled to himself. "The veil of my ignorance is so dark that I can't see any chink of light. This veil whispered to me once, though. A strange parable. Sightless remains the mind which can't grasp truth, and thoughtless remain the thoughts which avoid the tunnel of wisdom."

"What are your plans for the future?" Bryan got to his feet, his look distant.

"To write for the sake of sanity and income both." Gable elicited a smile, getting to his feet involuntarily.

"Both illusive and unpredictable." Bryan's sight strayed toward Ethel and Fabian.

"With this note of encouragement in my pocket, I must flee." Gable wanted to leave the adorable couple on the sofa.

"Must you leave so soon?" Ethel protested.

"You would visit us soon, won't you?" Fabian grasped Gable's hand warmly.

"Who cares if I ever visit or not." Bryan stalked away.

Fabian followed both friends, laughing, grabbing Bryan by the arm and slapping oaths of invitation right under his nose. Gable raced to his car, only his laughter trailing behind. Bryan was getting into his own car, uttering inanities.

"I need to save my sanity. Must see Lisa. I need her." Bryan's car was churning out of the driveway, oblivious to the cheerful waving of Fabian.

Seventeen ~ Maryana's Diary

The mute, amorphous dusk outside the Abbey was almost unreal, as Gable paced on the lawn like a lost spirit. He was troubled by the anxious look of the Superior Mother who had vanished behind the imposing doors, leaving behind this mysterious comment that Maryana needed a breath of fresh air more than her prayer and devotion. The maples and the crabapple trees in a blaze of fall colors were attracting his attention, and his feet came to an abrupt halt. His was drinking the nectar of beauty from the blush of pink and gold in leaves. So intense was his absorption that he didn't notice the approach of Maryana behind him.

"Who has robbed this monk of his wealth of gold?" Maryana whispered, infusing a note of light-hearted gaiety into her voice.

"Maryana." Gable swung around, facing the white ghost of a sister in nun's habit. "You are ill?"

"Have been ill, but now I am perfectly fine." Maryana lied, feeling the flames of damnation coiling inside her. "Come, walk with me." Her thin fingers clasped around Gable's arm. "Missed you so terribly. You are still handsome, even without your hair."

"What happened? When were you ill? Did you see a doctor? Why didn't anybody tell me?"

"Don't be such a child, Gable, nothing dreadful happened to me. Just a touch of cold and dyspepsia. Both gone now. Didn't tell mom and dad, they worry needlessly. We have a physician at the Abbey, very competent," She added, sealing the wound of spiritual leprosy within her with great care.

"How brave, Maryana, always playing the role of a martyr. You look more dead than alive, and I have this strange feeling that you're eager to embrace death." His thoughts were courting fantasy as if he was strolling beside a ghost.

"Death is peace, Gable, and bliss," Maryana said soothingly, buffeted by a sudden wave of pain which had become her living torment since her relationship with Reverend Valenty. "But that's a morbid subject, let's talk about life. We have a month of joyous anticipation. Davie is getting married. You would have a thatch of gold on your head by that time, and I would look healthy and beautiful."

"What is this obsession with all girls to look beautiful at the weddings?" Gable laughed, stumbling back to the rungs of reality, yet feeling a sting of premonition.

"This laughter, Gable. Somehow, is holding me by the hand and taking me back to the lazy summer days when we were young. Those days, how happy and carefree," Maryana said as if refreshing those memories this one last time.

"Have I grown that old, Maryana?" Gable could hear a dint of teasing in his voice. "I do feel old, though. Have been living for centuries, it seems, and not knowing why and what for? At least you know where you are, your heart pure and chaste. Piety, your peace and home." Awareness was dawning upon him that they were strolling back toward the Abbey.

"My heart is not as pure as you think." Maryana said with a sudden sinking of heart. "It is not safe from the flowers of corruption." She bit her lips, crushing the tapestry of sins inside her with clenched fists.

"Maryana." Gable stopped. "You are ill. Must come home."

"I am fine, Gable." Maryana smiled though a mist of tears. "I must go, this is my home." She fled before Gable could speak or move.

The lotus of karma, Gable thought.

***

Maryana was sitting in her bare cell like the one turned to a pillar of salt, her sins washed by the tears of agony and torture. The torture was self-inflicted as she had fallen into a fit of prayers and penance after abandoning Gable at the threshold of the Abbey. And this *agony* was her inner fountain of passion for Reverend Valenty which she could neither still, nor drain. The evening itself was drained into mournful silence, but Maryana's heart was still rumbling with the threat of a volcanic eruption. Finally, she had scrambled herself up, seeking the cold comfort of her chair. Seated at her rough desk, she had begun to write in her diary under a spell of fever and madness.

Are we not like those rare flowers which bloom against the wilderness of chance and adversity? Maryana's fingers were molding the words spoken by Valenty with the clarity of a devotee. *Yes, those unfortunate flowers, consumed by their own sense of beauty and innocence, never caring to behold their true reflections inside the mirror of time. Embracing death without sorrow and withering at the feet of destiny with joy and wild abandon.* Her fingers were numb and unwilling to mold more brands of fire which could lick her agony to cinders.

The funereal hush of the night was Maryana's only link to peace, and she was clinging to it with all her might, willing her thoughts to rest and sanity. The stern reproof of Mother Superior at her request for solitude was a distant echo in her mind and coming closer were the anguished notes of endearments from the heart of Valenty. An imperceptible shudder shook her whole inner being as she sat there listless, the memory of her sin and shame crawling forth to claim its rightful place inside the lacerated deeps of her very soul. The first time she had felt the shafts of love and torment from Reverend Valenty's lips and eyes was when he had found her weeping inside the secluded grove of the Abbey, all vulnerable and inconsolable.

Come, my child, wipe your tears away. Reverend Valenty had scooped her into his arms in one gust of a caress and consolation.

Maryana shuddered at this memory once again, this time shaking like a leaf, her forehead tingling with the unction of kisses he had imprinted in some shower of wild abandon. He was awesome and enchanting, cupping her face into his hands and murmuring endearments. She had thought then that she had seen the glory of God, alienated from the world of sorrow, and annihilated into the whirlpool of bliss. The tortures of the damned were to visit her later with the pincers of shame and guilt and they did in the seclusion of the night when she had lain on her bed trembling. Again and again, she was swept by the pain and paralysis of her passion for Reverend Valenty and more and more this god of illusion was absorbing her into his being. She was lost and condemned, heeding no storms, fighting no temptations. She thought she was dreaming, drifting toward the sweetness of a voice. Reverend Valenty had crept into the night of her pain and solitude. Alas, it was no dream, but a living torment.

"My love, I have frightened you."

"Valenty." A cry of pain was smothered in Maryana's throat, her features washed by some ethereal light of fear.

"My All." Reverend Valenty fell to his knees at her feet. "We must get married. Let me love, let me live." He claimed her hands, warming them with his kisses.

"Our love is wicked, we have sinned." Maryana closed her eyes against the glare of her shame and longing.

"My precious unforgettable," Reverend Valenty pleaded desperately. "How could this love such as ours so pure and sublime be wicked? Love is not a sin, but a blessing. God most merciful blesses and forgives the ones who love truly."

"I will be your death-bride." Maryana's voice was choked by the agony of her spirit, tears welling into her eyes.

"Hush, my love, hush." Reverend Valenty sealed her lips with kisses. "My virgin bride." He staggered to his feet. "You are tired and distraught. We would talk tomorrow." He turned to leave, "Sleep, my love. Peace and sweet dreams." He vanished behind the door.

Maryana kept sitting like a living corpse, her eyes drooping shut, and her mind wandering into the valleys of the blind and the leprous. Blind was her passion, coveting love in death. Leprous was her soul, longing to be cleansed by some miracle of mercy. Dreams and delusions were her tunnels of escape.

Yes, I would be wedded—to death. One prayer of a sob was seething in her dreams.

Eighteen ~ Agony of Friends

Gable, lolling on the couch in the parlor was lost in reveries, the only sound breaking silence was the pattering of rain against the French windows. He was looking out at the wet, shivering landscape. Six months had marched past with steam-engine haste since he had last seen Maryana. He was caught into a whirlwind of fame. His novel, *Black Robe*, on which he had been working for years, was finally published, lending his creative genius boost. Even this day, he had been at his desk all afternoon, scribbling away in feverish haste. Only a few minutes ago he had straggled down to the parlor for a breath of contemplation.

A mournful silence had settled into Gable's thoughts as he sat watching the gray evening with a poignant intensity. Ethel was looming in his mind as a remote constellation, adored and unapproachable. Visions of friends and family were hazy and illusive, Fabian was etched lanky in the distance, and Maryana slipping far past recognition. Davie's handsome face transfigured with joy was emerging forth as the beacon of love, and he was trying to imagine the star of his brother's devotion, Phoebe, whom he had met only through Davie's songs of praise and worship. Sorrow and loneliness were making themselves comfortable in his thoughts, and before he could admit their intrusion, he caught sight of the white Cadillac pulling into the driveway. Involuntarily, Gable sprang to his feet and rushed toward the door. Bryan had barely touched the doorbell, when Gable flung open the doors.

"What do I smell? It's definitely the odor of solitary confinement." Bryan sniffed, grunting a greeting and dashing straight toward the sofa.

"As long as the odor is clean and wholesome." Gable snorted with a stab at cheerfulness. "Mom and dad have gone shopping. They've been on shopping spree for months, hugging this precious excuse as Davie's wedding. And Davie, he's with his Phoebe, probably serenading her in some dimly-lit joint of magic and romance."

"And poor lonesome you." Bryan scoffed, leaning his head against the back of the sofa. "I thought the reek of piety would lure you back to the Temple of Gold, if not the incense of exaltation. Have you visited your sanctuary lately?" His tone was bitter and unfriendly.

"What exquisite blend of words you use to drain your own reek of anger or anguish," Gable declared with an attempt at soothing. "What made you presume that I would visit the Temple of Gold?"

"To see Lisa." Bryan said, as if scraping the rust out of his own heart. "You are *not* the one to abandon the intimate pleasures of a relationship"

"You presumptuous, little fool. What right do you have to interrogate the intimacy of our relationship?" Gable snapped with a sudden flaring of impatience.

"Lisa and I got engaged," Bryan blurted out this news.

"Congratulations." Gable laughed. "Fate has chained you to this link of love. If you get married soon, I promise you a grand reception."

"How intimate was your relationship with Lisa?" Bryan asked, his look distraught.

"Truth will sting you, Bryan, and you are welcome to strike me dead," Gable answered. "Intimate and distant both. Physically, much like the lovers, and mentally, gulfs apart."

"Love, lust, need, are they all not the same, donning the mantle of sanctity when caught under the noose of holy matrimony." Bryan muttered heedlessly, as if he had not heard Gable's confession.

"The epicurean in you, welcoming your own doom," Gable replied. "You are in love. Otherwise, you wouldn't be exposing your madness to pain and ridicule."

"Could the stoic in you teach me the art of stoicism?" Bryan appealed. "Yes, I must be in love. Jealousy kindling my heart to flames of rage. Madness indeed, that at times, I'm seized by this wild impulse to disfigure Lisa's face so that no one else could be tempted by her beauty, and I, worshipping her ugliness as my own gift of love and perfection."

"If I didn't know you, I'd be thinking I am talking to a madman." Gable looked into his eyes, more troubled than fascinated. "Maybe, you are mad. Nurturing such hideous thoughts."

"Even a prude like you fails to detect the subtlety of my passion." Bryan chuckled to himself.

"There is nothing subtle in men's passions as well as in their greeds and follies." Gable dared not laugh. "If there is any grain of sense left in you, hold on to your madness and you might discover joy."

"Joy in love, with a tinge of hatred at the bottom." Bryan lumbered to his feet, forlorn and indecisive.

"Hatred is the noblest of all passions without which the sweetness of love would go unnoticed with all its startling, astonishing affects." Gable spoke like the dialogue of a sickly protagonist in his new novel. "You are not leaving yet?"

"Most of us have to grind our way through the furnace of time to earn a living." Bryan was hurled out of his apathy in his flight toward the door.

"Find time to crawl your way to the church. When is the wedding?" Gable yelled.

"Soon, I hope. That way I don't have to rent the tux twice, can wear it for both weddings, mine and Davie's." Bryan's shower of hysteria was lost in the wind behind the closed doors.

Nineteen ~ Davie's Wedding

The wedding reception on the lawn of the Wittenberg chapel was brimming with music and laughter. Davie in blue tuxedo and Phoebe in lily-white gown beside his wheelchair were a rare sight of joy and beauty, radiating love as an offering of their own nuptial ceremony to the world around them. A beautiful world it was, the colors of autumn gilding the festivities with their own artistic décor, while the strings of lights twinkled with color of their own. The chefs, in starched liveries with silver trays balanced on their shoulders, were offering the guests a sumptuous feast as if vying with the waiters anxious to keep the wine glasses replenished.

Gable was not drinking much. One look at Phoebe with the face of an angel and his heart had sunk as if he had seen evil in the green goblets of her laughing eyes. She was beautiful, of course, much like a china doll in her precious fineries, but the gleam in her eyes was the *fire of fate*, boding evil at the very hearth of goodness. Gable had forced that vision out of his head, mixing with friends and family, his gaze wandering now and then in pursuit of Ethel. But the visions had left, his heart raw and aching, almost falling into the abyss of loneliness, where the joys of life could not enter.

Entering another phase of reverie and silence, he was whirled into the clouds of reality beyond imagination where *fear* was the *word* enveloping his sister and parents into the mantle of ill omens. He had just escaped the effusive embrace of a distant aunt and stood holding his wine glass, his sight landing on the round table where Maryana and his parents sat talking with other members of the family. His mom was smiling, but her features were washed by fatigue and sadness which he had failed to notice before. Mr. Faulkner had aged suddenly, it seemed, his complexion sallow, and wrinkles carving deep trenches around his lips and eyes. Maryana was seated next to him, pale and withdrawn, her eyes large and her lips shining like a red wound on her emaciated features.

She is dying. One lament of a revelation escaped Gable's thoughts, and he staggered aimlessly toward other tables.

The orchestra had struck a tune of the Vivaldi's Four Seasons, and Gable was lost in a world of beauty and enchantment. He was forcing his thoughts out of the dark tunnels and succeeding in claiming the light of joy and laughter all around. His heart lit up with the warmth of hope, as if kindling a lamp of joy to honor Davie's wedding with wit and revelry. Hope and eagerness were spontaneous since he had espied Ethel and was quick to join her, mischief and reverence now polishing his eyes to a bright sheen of the blue oceans.

"One loveliest of stars I have followed all evening. But it keeps drifting into its own shining orb and striking me blind." Gable laughed.

"The star of this evening is the lovely bride, bathed in the light of the sun, the handsome bridegroom." Ethel joined him in laughter.

"Davie is fortunate. My star is unattainable." Gable dared not voice his thoughts. "How is Kimberly? Haven't seen her in three whole days and it seems like centuries. Did she miss me?"

"Terribly," Ethel chanted, "You should be ashamed of yourself, neglecting her for so long."

"Tomorrow at the earliest, I would be on my knees, begging her forgiveness." Gable responded, his attention diverted to Maryana who drifted closer as if sleepwalking. "Maryana. You were supposed to look the best on Davie's wedding and look how you have taken care of your health." His arm closed around her waist. "Doesn't she look like a living corpse?" he said to Ethel.

"All bones and ether, I'm afraid."

Fabian had appeared on the scene like a ghost, his eyes arrested to Maryana. In fact, he had come looking for his wife, but finding Maryana in the semblance of a withered bloom, he stood stunned and speechless. His lips moved, no words coming to his rescue, seemingly oblivious to his wife and friend.

"You are breaking my bones with that stare, Fabian." Maryana chuckled. "Nuns are not supposed to look like well-fed matrons." She fled before anyone out of the trio could speak.

"I have been looking for you for the past half hour," Fabian said turning to Ethel.

"At weddings, the only person who could find his wife is the bridegroom," Gable said, summoning his sense of wit and propriety.

"Didn't see you. Must be seeing ghosts, and at weddings too," Fabian quipped, wrenching himself free from the spell of pain and shock. "Davie's bride is beautiful, isn't she?"

"Don't forget to mention to her that she has one handsome of a brother-in-law." Gable laughed, his expression embracing Lisa and Bryan who had emerged from behind the circle of merry guests.

"How very romantic and enchanting." Bryan sighed, pressing Lisa's hand and flashing smiles at all three friends.

"What is romantic and enchanting? Davie's marriage to Phoebe, or your engagement to Lisa?" Gable said.

"Both." Bryan slipped his arm around Lisa's waist.

"What do I hear, the wedding bells chiming again?" Ethel asked. "When is the wedding? Soon, I hope?"

"Seems quite far away, but she is arrested in my heart and can't escape." Bryan tipped his head in one gallant curtsy.

"Incarcerated, to use the proper expression. A helpless bird in a woebegone cage," Gable said while laughing.

"From one golden cage to the other, I suppose, since I have to abandon the Temple of Gold." Lisa replied.

"All I'm interested in is having a grand feast just like this one," Fabian added. "When is the happy feast day?"

"Our stars don't favor this century," Bryan quipped with a histrionic gesture. "Have to wait for this century to end."

"Lucky for you, coming this Saturday is the dawn of another century. Is that too long a wait?" Ethel said with a bright smile.

"Get married within a week and the reception is on me, remember?" Gable held Bryan captive with his piercing gaze.

"For sure. Yes, you will—"

Bryan's response was cut short by Mr. Faulkner's loud command to Gable, needing assistance with the gifts.

A mountain of gifts vanished into the vans as many more hands had come to Gable's assistance. The wedding feast had not lasted long due to Davie's express wishes because he couldn't participate in dancing. To Gable, the entire evening had melted into mists. But out of those mists, the face of his beloved was etched like a portrait torn straight out of his heart. This portrait was framed in the evening clouds as he drove his parents home, and *it* slipped into bed beside him as he shuddered under the blankets. Ethel's beauty—love's paradox, were lurking in his psyche like the colors of fate, the hands of nemesis poised over him like the merciless swords. He was exhausted and listless; the mute laws of his own suffering affording him the comfort of sleep.

Twenty ~ Death and Living Sins

Gable sat at his desk by the window, trying to concentrate on writing. He had not written much. The odor of death was still lingering in his mind over the past four years. So overwhelming was this reek in the sudden recollection of his *memory*, that he closed his eyes, as if shutting out the gates of the past with a curtain of darkness.

His body was inert, his head cupped into his hands, his eyes closed. Like a whirlwind, years were spinning inside the void of ether. He had been walking in a daze for the past four years, and now vague, incomprehensible shadows were stealing in through the back door of his mind, all tipsy and befuddled.

Maryana had committed suicide, his mom had died of grief and his dad had succumbed to death under the weight of *loss* and *loneliness*. The shock of Maryana's death, the grief of his parents, their deaths in succession left him immobile. Davie's hectic schedule away from home, Phoebe's charms, and his *Sin*. Gable's eyes shot open as fire shot through his heart like the tortures of hell and damnation. His lust and aberration, making love to Phoebe in the absence of Davie, were exploding inside him like a river corrupted. So overpowering was the smell of his own self-disgust and self-loathing that he leaped to his feet as if stung. He began to pace in his room, oblivious to the pincers of pain stinging his body and soul. His mind was reeling away from the tortures of sin and guilt, opening the diary of Maryana, its words burning like red hot coals inside the casket of his *memory*.

My love is like sweet poison, I have to drink it to the dregs before I die. Our whole family is cursed in the name of love, some sort of mad, noble paralysis of the—Gable's feet were coming to a stumbling halt before his desk, his gaze sucking in the lines of his villanelle which he had scribbled a few minutes ago.

Lost youth at the altar of ruins need not pray
To nemesis silent, sealed by God's holy decree
All thoughts are dunes of sand, and mind a pot of clay

Gable stood there leaning over his chair, feeling the eerie silence around him. His thoughts were loosening their hold on his guilt and self-loathing; reminding him about the true ache and longing inside him to see his beloved Ethel. Silence and loneliness were goading him to some sort of decision. He was plodding out of his room and edging closer to the staircase, becoming aware of the vast emptiness within. His mind itself was guiding him toward the home of his beloved, trying not to think about Davie who was having a romantic dinner with Phoebe in some grand hotel, blessedly ignorant of her liaison with the most despicable of scoundrels.

The evening had dwindled into the dull phantom of unreality as Gable reached Fabian's house. Ethel had gone shopping so he sat making paper boats with Kimberly while listening to the incessant news bulletin of Fabian. The soot of guilt in his thoughts had settled to a dull ache, his heart hoping to have a glimpse of his beloved. The memories which had attacked him were no more, but the odor of death was an imperceptible whiff in the air as if it was invading this very house where he sat talking with his friend.

"Lisa and Bryan are getting married, finally," Fabian said. He blinked away a flash of pain in the act of speaking, but no words coming to his lips.

"What's wrong, Fabian?" Gable watched him with concern and apprehension.

"Nothing. A little chest pain." Fabian's pallor was replaced by a sudden flush, a quick smile polishing the sherry brown in his eyes to gold. "I don't let that worry me, though people are dying right and left of heart attacks these days." He sipped his drink slowly and thoughtfully. "Too many to count, one of my neighbors, then my boss, another one of my colleagues. Is the world coming to an end, or something?"

"The curse of greed. This everlasting need to have money, more and more money. That's what's causing heart attacks, besides the blessings, rather, the abundance of food, and more food." Gable doubled the paper into a triangle for the benefit of Kimberly who was bent on constructing a fleet. "Don't underestimate this little chest pain, Fabian. See a doctor, or at least consult with Aslam," he suggested, absorbed in folding the paper into a conical shape. "He might give you little pills to relieve your little pain in your little chest." He smiled at Kimberly.

"Aslam is more in need of those little pills than me." Fabian laughed. "His stress is mounting high since his son started going to that Christian school, and the little fellow is only in kindergarten? 'My son has started talking like a Jesuit, already,' he says. Talking about stress, you're being buried alive under a mound, it seems. All this fame and writing? Take a break, get away. Now that you have enough royalties to live on, why don't you have a place of your own? Think about the future, what are your plans?"

"Don't have to think— future seems to have its own plans for me," Gable uttered as if to himself, his heart suddenly fluttering. "Can't move, Davie will feel devastated. Besides, I have grown attached to my room, my beautiful prison, a haven for writing."

"Well, if you wish to be a sentimental fool like that." Fabian shrugged his shoulders. "You're working on your new book, of course. What's the title? I forget."

"What a brilliant memory you have, Fabian. I haven't thought of the title yet," Gable responded.

"Besides writing, Gable, you should learn to live and enjoy life. You should—" Fabian's little pause was snatched by Gable.

"Think of getting married again?"

"Precisely," Fabian replied. "I've been saying that for the past six months. Also urging you to buy a house as your resolve toward getting married

"Are you talking about love, labor and chains of slavery, in marriage, that is?" Ethel said as she sprinted into the room. "Didn't even go shopping, met our neighbor right outside and have been visiting. Now, I must go on that planned shopping spree, since you two are bent on discussing everything dull and trite."

"Mom, look. Uncle Gable showed me how to make these boats." Kimberly scampered to her feet, scooping up her treasure of boats. "I want to go with you, Mom. Buy a big boat," she chirped innocently.

"Sure, you do, sweetie." Ethel laughed.

"Your wants have turned to needs, my dear, and we would surely go bankrupt," Fabian declared, joining Ethel in her laughter.

"Wants nurture needs, and needs feed on wants, both becoming inexorable," Gable commented, his heart sinking at the thought of Ethel leaving.

"Oh, these epigrams, I must flee." Ethel snatched Kimberly's hand into her own and turning she said, "We might file bankruptcy when I get back."

"Women are not only unpredictable, but restless and misguided," Fabian said solemnly after Ethel and Kimberly had left.

"You sound so suddenly morbid," Gable said.

"I was thinking about Maryana," Fabian responded.

"I try not to think about that," Gable answered.

"What makes one despise one's own life?" Fabian continued heedlessly.

"Helpless, hopeless pain of living, I guess," Gable said with a stoic reserve. "But let's not talk about it."

"Did you read in the newspaper that Reverend Valenty also committed ...." Fabian stopped, becoming aware of the pain in Gable's eyes.

"Don't read newspapers anymore." Gable contrived a smile. "Trying my best to stay away from the ills of sensationalism. I have enough inside me to keep me occupied, my follies, my madness'."

"It is healthy to keep in touch with the madness' of others, sometimes," Fabian demurred aloud. "You will forget about your follies once you're married."

"I was married once, remember?" Gable elicited one pale smile. "Strange, lovely mates. Madness all."

"We can all fit in that box of strange and lovely. You, me, Bryan, even Davie." Fabian couldn't slough off this vague feeling of madness within him.

"I wouldn't put Bryan in the same box." Gable got to his feet.

"Bryan thinks he is in love. Isn't this reason enough for madness?" Fabian's look was puzzled.

"Don't we all think we are? But I must leave before I'm swallowed by this thought unfathomable." Gable turned on his heels to leave.

"Won't you stay for dinner, Ethel would be disappointed?" Fabian said, looking lost and forlorn.

"Not as much as I," Gable said as he waved goodbye.

Twenty-One ~ Road to Fame

If only madness could cease, if only hope could materialize. One impudent thought was materializing in Gable's head this autumnal evening with all its glory of colors in saffron and vermilion.

This was the eve of Lisa and Bryan's wedding reception, revealing its splendor on the lawns of the Masonic temple where the guests had gathered around the round tables with white table-cloths and sparkling silver. Gable was standing near the table where Davie and Phoebe were seated with the other guests. The large floral arrangement before his gaze was changing colors in conformity with his thoughts, though he stood listening to the merry guests, seemingly avid and attentive. This very day he had heard from his publisher about the book tour for his new book with the prospect of making millions. This was not the only reason for his surge of elation. He could now live in the dream-world with his beloved regardless of the burden of reality which suffered the tortures of longing and separation.

Gable's senses were tied to the dreamlike *vision of a world* where his lusts in life and tragedies past and present were dissolved into a pool of nothingness. He had even surrendered to the hurricanes of sin and adultery as if obeying the commands of fate. No more resisting the requests of Davie to entertain Phoebe while he was on tours. Only one canker of a reality within him which he could neither dissolve, nor obliterate was his formidable hunger for the purity of love which only Ethel would ever be able to feed and satisfy, if fates favored his dreams and madness'. He just wanted to gaze at his beloved and to fill his lungs with the music of her voice, as if no one else were present but the essence of *her* beauty and perfume. He was jolted out of his reveries, though, as Bryan approached him.

"How dare you look more handsome than the groom?" Bryan drained his wine in one gulp. "How long has it been since we drank ourselves to oblivion?"

"Not long for me, and this evening might afford another opportunity," Gable responded, noticing Fabian's swift approach.

"Come and sit at our table." Fabian sought Gable's attention with an imperious wave of his arm. "Leave this Bedouin of a bridegroom alone to his own schemes; he's been drinking since two in the afternoon!"

"What an insensitive pack of friends I have. Have you congratulated me?" Bryan turned to Fabian, his face brimming with merriment.

"Ten times over. Though, you wouldn't remember." Fabian laughed.

"The wine of wedlock has gone to his head," Ethel chimed in.

"Not to mention the grape wine." Davie's own banter rippled over the sea of gaiety and laughter.

"The bride is lovelier than a dream." This comment from one young man's lips floated after Lisa as she joined the merry group.

"You are adorable and irresistible." Bryan caught Lisa into his arms and sprinted away to the beat of the music under the cloud of inebriation.

Gable lit a cigarette and plodded toward the table where Ethel and Fabian had joined Davie and Phoebe. He sank into a chair next to Davie, discomfited by a barrage of complaints from his brother in neglecting Phoebe when he was away performing in other cities or states. Phoebe was defending Gable most charmingly, almost gloating with joy that Davie was leaving for another concert this evening, affording her the freedom of much cherished moments with Gable. Gable was half listening, half dreaming, the ache of loneliness inside him throbbing. His eyes rested on Ethel with tenderness and longing. So deeply immersed was he in his lonesome retreat that he had failed to notice Davie's leave-taking, sinking deeper and deeper into the desert of his own inner silence. He was merely content to be in the company of his beloved. Fabian waved his hand before his eyes.

"Where are you, Gable?" Fabian demanded hilariously. "Shut off the gates of your dreams and come back to us."

"Sorry."

"My compliments about your new novel have gone down the drain since you were not listening." Fabian smiled, making sure that he has his friend's attention. "Now follows the critique. Your characters, though dull and remote, have a flair for revealing their agonies, though they keep their joys guarded."

"Agonies of the soul, my besotted critic, have a million cries to silence, while the joys in hearts are rigged with pain to be guarded," Gable said. "Pain is the kernel of life, lending voice to both joy and agony, without it nothing can be felt or experienced."

"Joy has its own tongue to sing its songs, it doesn't need the Babel of pain to voice its ecstasy," Fabian teased poetically.

"Oh, these endless epigrams," Ethel exclaimed.

"I agree with Ethel. This kind of talk is absolutely insane," Phoebe said.

"The purpose of life is to attain joy, and the presence of pain makes no sense, does it?" Fabian prodded Gable, heedless of the protests from the ladies.

"The sense of pain is in ambition, aspiration, inspiration, without which nothing could be achieved," Gable replied without interest.

"How terrible to justify pain in such a fashion." Phoebe tried to claim Gable's attention.

"Much too bleak an argument for my health." Ethel said.

"What is there in suffering?" Fabian was explaining to no one in particular.

Gable sat listening, trying to participate in gaiety and laughter. Paradoxically, he was sucked into the vortex of his own oblivion where Ethel alone was *time, love, eternity*. The canker of longing inside him had bloated to the size of an ocean from where there was no escape, except for death and annihilation. So profoundly arrested was he in this that he had no idea how and when he had driven Phoebe home until he stood in the parlor in some sort of shock.

"Why don't you sit down and relax? I don't bite." Phoebe cooed her usual appeal in finding herself alone with Gable. "Davie won't be home for another couple of hours." She flung herself on the couch, flashing a disdainful look at the oppressive furnishings. "I know you hate me. But couldn't you coat your hatred in a thin layer of love?" She laughed.

"If it was in my power, I would efface the word *love* from the dictionary of human folly," Gable said, anger swelling inside him with the hiss of a serpent.

"On second thought, I know you love me," Phoebe purred deliciously. "Yes. Love, without joy, passion or pleasure," she confessed, her eyes sparkling with adoration.

"I couldn't have expressed it more explicitly." Gable managed to unglue his feet in an act of pacing.

"Are you capable of loving anyone? Truly, I mean?" Phoebe asked, her eyes following him in his slow, deliberate pacing.

"Love is not capable of holding even one grain of truth in its ocean of lies, my lovely she-devil," Gable exclaimed with a sudden vehemence. "Love is either wickedly good, or sweetly corrupt."

"In that case, I want to be loved by you sweetly and wickedly."

"I couldn't love you any other way," Gable replied.

"No matter what you say about love, true or false, wicked or corrupt, you are possessed by it. Unfortunately, it's not me. Who is the lucky one?" Phoebe goaded relentlessly.

"Are you tempting me to provoke your jealousy?" Gable said.

"So very touching to think about my jealousy," she said. "Don't you trust me?"

"Trust is an odious word, even from the lips of a she-devil. Even the reek of my own breath dares not trust the word, reek."

"Let me be the judge of your breath. I have experienced only sweetness, time and time again." Phoebe closed her eyes.

"You have no guilt, no shame," Gable uttered as if to himself. "As vile and doomed as me."

"Not vile, just a beautiful puzzle I am, even to myself." Phoebe opened her eyes, the smoldering flames in them bright with longings. "And yet, nothing complex about me. You could look right into my soul if you wanted."

"Somehow, I lack the courage to look into the mirror-image of my own soul, bleak and damned." Gable's feet came to an abrupt halt, his look glazed and murderous. "Good night, dear temptress."

"You can't shut yourself in your room yet, Gable." Phoebe sprang to her feet. "Not until you tell me the name of your love, true or false."

"If you insist." Gable crushed her into his arms savagely. "Ethel." One agony of a confession escaped his lips which were sealed upon hers with the hunger of pain and insanity.

Twenty-Two ~ Dewdrop Illusions

The gold-gray evening, much like the dusk of age in Gable's hair, lingered outside in utmost silence as he sat with Ethel and Fabian inside their living-room, talking and laughing. Eons. Perhaps, centuries had swirled past as far as Gable was concerned, and he was still waiting for the hearth of love at the feet of his beloved. He had aged, though Ethel had not changed much, and Kimberly was transformed into a teenage blossom, avid and sprightful. Gable could feel his thoughts rippling inside the muddied waters of the past, though he sat listening to Fabian, blissfully content for the nearness of Ethel. His lust for Phoebe, his love for Ethel, and his obsession with writing were rolled into paper-thin layers of time. He had no time to behold the jungle of vice and corruption inside him while cultivating the flowers of love in words and thoughts. But he was becoming aware of Fabian's fiery criticism, directed toward his new novel.

"What strange passions haunt the characters in your new book, I'm not sure, but I am beginning to like your style." Fabian was in a generous mood to unleash his string of compliments. "What an ocean of agony and ecstasy in their hearts, shining with the wealth of gold when touched by your genius." He laughed.

"That wealth, my fair critic, is nothing but a reed of imagination, woven tight into knots of absurdities." Gable joined him in laughter, draining his share of whiskey in one quick gulp. "Those characters, too, as soon they leave my mind, are cold as death, happy to be in their graves."

"Some special graves. Bursting open with applause and making you wealthy." Fabian's mirth was uncontrollable.

"Wealth, my friend, digs its own graves of agonies and ecstasies which seem dead along with the characters. But I won't elaborate on that since Ethel is finding our conversation dull, if not totally absurd." Gable stole a glance at Ethel.

"Wrong, Gable, you do me injustice," Ethel quickly protested. "I find your conversations most charming, especially when you both dig through the rubble of characters, dead or alive." She got to her feet. "I would love to stay, but have to drop Kimberly at her friend's, then shoot for the meeting at our church, talking of dull and a little absurd, too."

"Don't tell me you don't enjoy such meetings?" Fabian teased, his gaze caressing Kimberly who had just sailed into the room.

"Hello, uncle." Kimberly greeted Gable before turning to her mother. "May I drive, please, let me?" She pleaded.

"Do a small favor to your old uncle, Kimberly," Gable interceded. "Accept my old car as a gift, and then you would have the luxury of driving, and freedom."

"How could you suggest such a thing, Gable? Such an expensive gift to a teenager." Ethel was incredulous.

"That old car as you say, Gable, is Cadillac, only a year old," Fabian declared.

"Please Mom. Please Dad." Kimberly jumped with excitement. "Uncle is only lending me the car. I would return it when you could buy me one."

"Your behavior is unbecoming, young lady, you must practice restraint," Fabian admonished. "No need to discuss this any further."

"Come, dear, you are welcome to have the Mercedes on my dresser." Ethel laughed, dragging her daughter along, out of the room.

"Don't you think you are too hard on Kimberly, Fabian?" Gable asked, lighting another cigarette. "She needs a car, and I happen to have one, nothing wrong in using it, otherwise, it would sit idle in the garage, collecting dust, if not rust. Kimberly is like a daughter to me, and you would be robbing me of the joy of making her happy, if you don't let her accept this gift."

"She would be living in a castle of gold, if it was in your power." Fabian could not help laughing. "Her room is full of precious gifts from you, every time you come, you bring her one. Wonder, why you didn't bring any this evening? If the burden of money is robbing you of your sleep, spend it wisely, a grand mansion, perhaps."

"Mansions, those monuments of ugliness. Why would I want to live in one?" Gable watched the ring of smoke he had just made. "As for the gift this evening, a worthless one, I did offer, but you forbid her to accept."

"I wouldn't be your friend, Gable, if I took advantage of your generosity, please try to understand." Fabian began thoughtfully, "You need to settle down and have a home. Maybe Davie and Phoebe need their privacy, have you ever thought about that? Moreover, you can find an outlet for your royalties by purchasing a decent home."

"I wanted to leave after mother passed away, but Davie clung to me like a child." Gable said. "Every time I voice my intention of leaving he starts crying and imploring. Well, our memories together, and something more powerful than sentiment, I can't explain."

"Sorry, didn't mean to stir the memories of loss and grief." Fabian breathed contritely. "I wish, rather dream, you living in a quaint, little home of your own, a wife, and children." He paused. "Don't you feel lonely at times, the absence of love, family life? You have money, friends, even notoriety, but don't you feel something missing in your life, something you'd like to possess to claim as your own, a cat maybe, or a dog, even a mistress?"

"Can one truly claim to possess *anything*?" Gable declared. "Wedded to my evil thoughts, I am. All these thoughts are molded into one, my *sinful bride*, whom I possess completely, and am in return possessed by *her*. Only our follies and madness' are our sole possessions, don't you think? We are not the masters of our will, as we would like to believe, but its slaves. This paradox of owning, possessing and patching the vacuums in our lives with things, relationships, *stuff*? Wives and husbands, another paradox. Two parallel lines marked by selfishness, following their own separate paths, never meeting, forever groping in the dark for a tryst which could never be."

"A steam-engine philosophy of yours which fails to shock me anymore." Fabian responded. "If you are thinking about the stormy marriage of Lisa and Bryan, ending in, well, that alone can't be the measure of judging all marriages. Take ours, for example, we're happy."

"Truly, Fabian, you can't be that naïve, happiness doesn't exist." Gable's look was piercing. "A meaningless word."

"To you, Gable, the whole wide world is a cauldron of misery and suffering. Joy doesn't exist," Fabian said.

"It does, my friend, in contrast to pain. You would have to experience both to distinguish one from the other." Gable smiled, caught in his own net of contradictions. *Light reveals both itself and darkness*, didn't Spinoza write that? And yet, all thoughts and emotions are perceptions, reflecting illusions and revealing nothing." He couldn't continue, noticing his friend's sudden pallor, as if all blood had drained from his face. "What's wrong, Fabian?"

"This pain in my chest, it's gone now." Fabian sighed relief, his cheeks now flushed. "I have had it for some time now, but it leaves as quickly as it comes."

"You must see a doctor, Fabian," Gable suggested with an abrupt vehemence. "Condoning it won't solve the problem."

"How I detest doctors, more than medicines," Fabian protested. "Psychiatrists, I don't mind, they inspire my curiosity. But doctors, they fill me with dread."

"Doctors are not a pack of wolves, Fabian. They're not going to tear you up and devour." Gable laughed. "The joy of health would be worth taking a few detestable pills, and they might—"

Ethel sailed into the room. "The meeting was cancelled." Ethel said, her gaze fixed to the flushed cheeks of her husband. "You're having those awful pains again, I can tell, Fabian. You can't protest anymore, I must call the doctor."

"This child needs strict discipline, Ethel," Gable commented before Fabian could protest. "I must leave while you make this important call." He got to his feet.

"No, you can't!" Fabian leaped to his feet with a sudden alacrity.

"Please stay." Ethel smiled, the dazzling-blue in her eyes perceptive and piercing.

"I'd love to, but I can't," Gable said, turning abruptly. "Don't let Fabian persuade you to postpone this call, Ethel. Good-bye and good luck."

The fiery sunset was gilding the landscape to a coppery sheen as Gable drove past the commercial area onto the interstate. He was driving aimlessly, heading for no particular destination, obeying only the dictates of his thoughts, on the verge of rebellion. Some sort of hope was a shining mirage in his psyche. He could even hear the fates laughing in the background. Somewhere, the bubble of cosmic glory was ticking away its pulse of reality and illusion. Terrible and relentless, time was merging into timelessness. Ethel was there, too, young and adorable, welcoming him into her radiant eyes, heart, soul. His own soul was on fire, reflecting his sin, and holding him captive inside the pincers of agony where he was wont to suffer the tortures of the damned. He himself had no recollection as to when he had taken the exit, forking into an arena of shops, parks, and one sliver of a bike route.

Guided more by the agony of his spirit, than by his need to contemplate, Gable had parked his car and had begun strolling amidst the stream of walkers and joggers. Oblivious to the ocean of humanity all around, his thoughts were inward bound, succumbing to the sense of loneliness. He was becoming the victim of a profound sadness so palpitating that he could actually breathe the pain. The sigh of despair was in the wind, filling the vacuum of the night sky with laments. He was a part of this dream-world, living a dream, and fascinated by the dark mists in dreams, where thoughts whirled and screamed, longing to assert their personality as the throne of reality.

How could I ever divorce the bride of my solitude, and seek the abode of bondage in marriage? Gable was becoming aware of the crunching of leaves under his feet, his thoughts picking speed with the sudden gusts of wind. *Creatures of the wind. How very much like these leaves is the spirit of man, restless and will-less, whipped by forces invisible and fathomless. Fallen is the state of man, in conformity with nature, on the verge of death and disintegration. Can one die pure and whole, retaining the innocence and freshness of childhood, free from the rust of sins and corruptions? This world, our Eden of deformities. Is there no balm for the festering wounds inside me to heal and cauterize? Could Phoebe ever become faithful to Davie? Would I ever stop longing for my beloved? Must I kill my dream? How to escape this snarling den of madness—home? Suffer I must, my sin, my lust for Phoebe, this torture.*

"I am not thin air, young man that you can slice right through me." The stranger, with whom Gable had collided, waved at him menacingly.

"Sorry. Forgive me." Gable was focusing his thoughts in locating his car.

The delirious night with dreams inviolate was dissolved into tear-streaked morning with billowing clouds as Gable sat at the breakfast table with Davie and Phoebe. Davie was trying to swallow his omelet as Phoebe was sipping her coffee daintily, her gaze wandering aimlessly.

"Guess, who came awfully late last night?" Phoebe asked, flashing a radiant smile. "Where did you go, Gable?"

"Met old friends," Gable said. "A few drinks and wild arguments, don't remember a thing."

"The pleasure of having breakfast at home." Davie protested suddenly. "This toast tastes like sand, and the omelet, well—"

"Darling, I am so sorry," Phoebe interrupted. "The cook didn't show up this morning. "You've spoiled me, Davie. I haven't fixed breakfast since we got married."

"Besides being spoiled, sweetheart, you are lucky." Davie laughed. "I have no engagements today, and we would go out to lunch." His look was shifting to his brother. "These long hours of writing are taking a toll on you, Gable, how pale you look. You must have lunch with us and get away from your prison of a solitary confinement."

"Sorry, Davie, that's not possible, not today." Gable smiled. "I have a deadline, and the task of editing those stories is daunting."

"Please don't shut yourself up in your study again," Phoebe pleaded.

"Sorry, dear, this is the only way to get my work done." Gable stumbled to his feet. "A perfect day for you two to be alone. Together, free of intrusion from your brother."

"The great intruder is excused," Davie quipped. "Since you prefer your solitary confinement, it would indeed be a good day to spend some time with my wife. I rarely get time to spend with any one of you." A shadow of pain crossed his features as he turned his attention to his wife. "As soon as you get dressed, darling, we would be on our way to gallivant wherever."

"Dressed for show-time, it would only take me a few minutes." Phoebe skipped to her feet, pirouetting her way out of the room.

"You've grown so dull and listless, Gable." Davie's look was sad. "Can't figure out what's wrong with you? You're suffering, it is obvious, some sort of inward struggle I guess. You have money, you're successful, and yet? What you lack is love, the need to love and being loved in return. You must fall in love and get married."

"The love of a wife, my child-brother, is nothing but a mockery of love itself." Gable began with an abrupt vehemence. "One should not ever marry; especially, if one loves truly, the worthy victim of love surrendering one's heart and soul to the beloved incarnate. I was married once, remember. How beautifully I inspired hatred into the heart of my wife, how admirable. I'm in the habit of repeating my follies, but the folly of getting married I dare not repeat."

"Your world of illusion, Gable," Davie said. "You've closed shut the doors of reality and live amidst the mists of your bookish characters who mimic passions but can't feel them, not ever tasting the bitter-sweet joys of living, giving and sharing. Those lifeless, soulless characters are holding you prisoner, Gable. Steer clear out of that world and you would learn to live and love."

"My handsome musician, the symphony of your expression can breathe life into words if you but tried your hand at writing," Gable said. "Those lifeless characters as you deem them to be have a life of their own. They reveal our own passions of love and hate, of lusts and greeds, the emblems of our failures and triumphs. Words have life, Davie, they are the pulse of life, a spark of reality most subtle, terrible and palpitating. Words are our angels and demons, pregnant with the soma of reality, and sheltered by the clouds of illusions."

"You need to exorcise your demon, Gable, before you can get to your angel," Davie replied.

"*Be careful, lest in casting out the devil, you might cast out the best, that's in you.* Gable quoted Nietzsche, laughing to himself. "In this world of reality, I might let the devil in me have the upper hand, but the angels in my dreams make me soar beyond harm and ugliness."

"One day you would wake up ugly and wrinkled, Gable, lonely as ever, the sting of reality stabbing that you wasted your youth and talents, rejecting the pleasures of love and family. What is your aim in life, have you ever thought?"

"The aim in life, for everyone, Davie, is simple, just to live," Gable responded emphatically.

"How simple could it get? You have chosen simply, not to live," Davie replied regretfully, watching Phoebe, sailing down the winding staircase.

"Well, don't I look stunning?" Phoebe asked.

"Yes, an artist's dream!" Davie complimented, returning his attention to his brother. "Return to your prison, Gable, but don't forget to eat."

"Cleaning lady should be coming soon. She'd be delighted to fix you a sandwich, Gable," Phoebe added.

"Thank you," Gable said, turning abruptly, not even noticing that Davie had wheeled his chair out of the room, Phoebe following.

Seated at his desk in the study, Gable was lost into a pool of silence, only his thoughts trickling down words on blank pages, all dull and lifeless. He was chain-smoking and writing feverishly. His mind was a whirlpool of madness, churning tides upon tides of memories where Ethel was his Muse, the beloved dream, his only link to pain and sanity. Hope was there, too, woven around his altar of bliss like a beautiful garland, waiting for the beloved to come, repeating but one name, uttering but one prayer, Ethel, Ethel. Shame and despair were not far behind either, his soul aghast and anguished. So profoundly immersed was he in the fantastic downpour of his words that he didn't hear the cleaning lady until she knocked twice.

"I'm done cleaning, would you want me to clean your room before I leave?" The cleaning lady ventured forth, without being invited into the room.

"Next week, perhaps," Gable said over his shoulders, forcing his concentration back to writing.

Like the one possessed, Gable kept writing, his thoughts whirling and somersaulting. Stacks upon stacks of papers were blackened with dreams, reveries and a collage of imaginations, all wild and phantasmagoric, and still he kept writing. Delirium and madness were with him and darkness, too. He was oblivious to the pale, glimmering shadows of the evening which had crept into his study, demanding his attention. Suddenly, the darkness within him was splintering, his mind pleading rest, and his limbs sagging under the weight of fatigue. He was too wearied to write, too wearied to turn on the light, too wearied to think. His soul was silent and simmering. Something inside him was famished, not the physical hunger gnawing at his stomach, but the hunger of the soul, longing for love.

Agony of the spirit was Gable's pillow as he flung himself upon the bed, but arms of sleep were cradling him into the blanket of dreams. He was drifting deep into the innocence of childhood and passions of youth. Much like the phantoms of ice and fire, his family and friends were materializing inside the bowers of his sleep. Davie and Phoebe, Fabian and Kimberly, Lisa, Aslam, Heather, all and many more were emerging forth like the troubadours, singing the Legend of Greece. Dedalus was hovering above in mists gossamer, and he was the unfortunate son, Icarus, his wings of wax melting, his body turning to one grotesque lump of charred flesh and hurled into some abyss, dark and bottomless. Davie was enacting the part of Icarus next, then Fabian, both swallowed by the abysmal deeps unfathomable. Gable was the spectator now, standing rapt and dazzled, watching the unfolding of a miracle. Ethel robed in the purity of light was rising above the mists, the *bride of nature*, inviting him, the bridegroom, to join her, to reclaim the long-lost joys of love and youth.

Ethel, the *lost bride*, was smiling, the fragrance of her breath reaching him, sweet and intoxicating. He was frozen in time, the vacuum between him and his beloved a gulf of separation. But he could not reach his bride, all mists were shattering, the horror of loneliness returning. Nothing was left but the roaring ocean of pain and silence. Love was a *pearl of reality* inside the abysmal deeps of his dreams, but he couldn't reach it, his heart a cauldron of torture and longing. Fate was confronting him, tossing its own blanket of hopelessness and hope was gone, beauty effaced.

Twenty-Three ~ Shadow of Death

"Why all this gloom, my friends? I know I haven't seen you for two whole months, but I was hoping for a warm welcome." Gable assumed a cheerful expression as Ethel and Fabian led him into their living room. "Did you two have a fight and can't figure out exactly how to compromise?" He sank down beside Fabian on the sofa, while Ethel settled herself on the rocker, eliciting a pale smile.

"Fights are good for a healthy, happy marriage." Fabian's laugh was hollow and artificial. "Ethel here fears that I'm going to die. All doctor's fault, I say, since he made the diagnosis. Some sort of tumor under my neck, the size of a pea. Can be removed easily I've been told, but Ethel doesn't trust the surgeons."

"Sorry, I didn't know," Gable said softly, feeling a stab of pain in the pit of his stomach.

"You too, my stoic friend, have premonition of my death?" Fabian said, concealing his own fears.

"After the surgery, you'd be a paragon of health," Gable replied. "My concern is for Ethel, not for you."

"Thanks for caring … for me," quipped Fabian. "For a minute I thought you were concerned about my health."

"Have you finished your new novel yet?" Ethel was quick to change the subject, fleeing the turmoil inside her own thoughts.

"Almost, but the last chapter doesn't seem to budge." Gable was relieved to divert his thoughts, also.

"You mean you went into seclusion for two long months for nothing. Shame on you for neglecting us and not even reaching the finish line as intended," Fabian chided. "Didn't you miss us, your dearest of friends?"

"Terribly. Especially, Kimberly," Gable intoned. "My solitary confinement, as Davie calls it, gilded with the fever of urgency, doesn't permit any sane ending. The truth is, I get lost in dreams and forget that I need to write."

"Would you care sharing some of your dreams with us?" Fabian asked. "I'm as good as the Daniel of Biblical times and very adept in offering interpretations."

"Yes, he truly is a dream-dictionary," Ethel commented with a sudden cheerfulness. "Though his interpretations are wired to the wrong signals."

"I don't claim to be the Nebuchadnezzar, so you don't need to fear your head being chopped off, Fabian, if you make a wrong interpretation," Gable retorted. "My dreams are mundane, following Cinderella's footsteps, happily ever after, if that's the right expression."

"One of these days, Gable, you're going to find your Cinderella," Ethel said as she got to her feet. "But at the moment, a feast is waiting for you, T-bone steaks and potato casserole must be sizzling in the oven by now." She glided out of the room without waiting for any comments.

"Why don't you give voice to your dreams, Gable, they might fall into the tub of reality?" Fabian goaded.

"A tub of reality drained of all magic and mystery." Gable avoided the intensity in his friend's gaze by lighting a cigarette.

"Even your epigrams are getting dull by the minute." A snort of laughter escaped Fabian's lips, his eyes shining at the sudden appearance of his daughter and her friend, Steve.

"You save this kind of laughter only for Uncle Gable, Dad," Kimberly protested happily, introducing Steve to Gable.

"So very glad to meet you, Steve." Gable shook his hand warmly, feeling a subtle pang, as if his own daughter was being claimed by another.

"Steve is doing his residency at the River Side, Gable." Fabian said. "Let us hear your comments about medical profession, you so highly praise and revile?" He indicated a seat to Steve, while Kimberly abandoned herself on the sofa between Gable and Fabian.

"Doctors and soldiers are the only enviable professionals, getting paid for hurting and killing." Gable laughed.

"Sorry, I asked." Fabian shifted his attention to Steve. "Don't pay any attention to my maverick friend here, his ideas corrupt young minds."

"Dad," Kimberly said. "Dad and uncle always get into this *idle pleasure*, as they call it, of sharing ideas, if not getting into arguments. But it is fun listening to them."

"Both enlightening and entertaining, I feel." Steve smiled, rising to his feet as Ethel sailed into the room.

"I was wondering at the light of joy flooding my kitchen and now I know why." Ethel smiled, greeting Steve profusely.

"That means, Steve can stay for dinner, Mom?" Kimberly teased.

"Of course, honey, he doesn't need an invitation to share a meal with us."

"I hope I'm not imposing."

"The delight of sharing a meal with any of my daughter's friends can never be an imposition, always a delight." Ethel flashed him a bright smile. "Be quick to bring everyone to the dining room, Fabian, or you'll be eating charcoal instead of steaks

The chandelier was dimly lit, absorbing light from the candles, as all sat down to dinner, the course of parlance as delicious as the viands skillfully cooked and garnished. Steve was enjoying the food and the conversation with a sense of euphoria, his own wit matching the syllogisms of Gable and Fabian. Ethel was just content to be the hostess, forgetting to eat, and not even noticing that Kimberly was watching her apprehensively.

"You haven't touched your food, Mom." Kimberly sought her mom's attention abruptly. "You look pale. Are you all right?"

"A slight headache, that's all." Ethel smiled. "You know your mom. I get so engrossed in listening to everyone that I forget to eat."

"Am I the only glutton around here?" Fabian caught that comment and smiled at his wife. "Thank you, dear, for this scrumptious dinner."

"The best I've had in months." Steve tossed his own compliment, cutting another chunk from his steak.

"The best cook in the world, that's my mom," Kimberly sang passionately.

The magic of the evening and his beloved Ethel were left behind as Gable drove home, his thoughts all befuddled as to how long he had stayed, or when he had left. The bubble of time was punctured in his head, forcing open the eyes of fate. He could feel the hand of destiny, pushing him deeper into the abyss of hopelessness.

Fabian may not live long? Ethel could be mine? Would she not grieve? God, what madness is this, let Fabian live. Heal my wounds, God, forgive. Oh, forgive, beloved, for carving hope out of your own grief. Forgive this madman, Ethel, forgive. Gable's thoughts were silent as he parked his car, drifting straight into the prison of his home.

"Welcome home, sweet tyrant." Phoebe sang, from where she lounged on the couch, hugging her robe to herself.

Gable came to an abrupt halt in the middle of the parlor. He could neither speak, nor move; the churning of pain and desire inside him one volcanic hunger. *She-devil is watching him*, his thoughts were hissing, billowing up into a whirlwind of agony and hysteria.

"Have no fear, darling, Davie is not coming home tonight," Phoebe said with a mingling of malice and coquetry. "By the look in your eyes I can tell you're returning from the shrine of your beloved. You don't have to say a word, just make love to me and I will forgive everything."

"Has it ever occurred to you, Phoebe, that in my heart of hearts, your vile charms are repulsive and hateful?" Gable stood his ground, oblivious to his inner torment which had spewed forth this expression.

"My idol of perfidy, darling, you are my pain and bliss both, I might as well confess, this strange evening." Phoebe laughed. "You will never be able to resist my charms, Gable, and my beauty would haunt you forever, even after death."

"Our sin itself, Phoebe, would cut us apart, if not my own sin, lust and disgust," Gable declared, turning to his heels. "Dare not follow me, Phoebe, if you hold your life dear." He flung this challenge while mounting the staircase as if pursued by the demons.

***

Time had become the serpent of fall and expulsion, crawling endlessly, and getting further away from its ocean of destiny. That's how Gable was feeling this evening as he drove toward the home of his friends. He had not seen Ethel and Fabian for two whole months, immuring himself inside the jungle of his writing when not busy promoting his books. Always longing to see them, but dreading the trumpets of inevitability which might announce the hour of death, flooding his heart and the heart of his beloved with the agony of loss and grief.

Love is a lie, and hatred the kernel of truth. Falsely we love, and truly we nurture the seeds of hatred. The splinters of dull wit were piercing Gable's thoughts, as he pulled his car into the driveway.

"Uncle Gable. I missed you." Kimberly flew into Gable's arms as Fabian led him into the dining room, Ethel greeting him with a pale smile.

"Had I known that, my dear, I would've whipped myself away from work and tours." Gable held her before him, searching her eyes.

"Don't just stand there, darling, get a plate and silver for your uncle, he looks famished," Ethel chided Kimberly.

Kimberly fled without a word, as his keen senses absorbed all the gloom and doom which pervaded the dining room. The air itself was charged with a sense of mourning as Gable seated himself beside Fabian, daring not to meet Ethel's gaze, where the pools of sparkling blue were tainted with sadness. Kimberly returned with a plate and silver and placed it before him, returning to her seat with a sigh as if fighting a flood of tears.

"Our joy is so very contagious, isn't it, Gable?" Fabian began sarcastically. "You must be wondering why we are looking so sad and gloomy. Well, the truth is, I have cancer of the liver. The tumor was successfully removed, if you didn't know. The new test results came this afternoon." He couldn't continue, noticing the mists of tears flooding his wife and daughter.

"Sorry, dear," Ethel murmured, drying her tears with her napkin.

"Tears will wash away your fears, dear Ethel," Fabian consoled. "Tears and smiles, I get from my family. And what do I get from my childhood friend? Only a frown? Relax, Gable, this accursed frown makes you look hideous and may mar your face forever into permanent wrinkles." He laughed more so to drown his own fears than to wash clean the fears of his friend and family.

"A test of your great friendship, Fabian, if you could stay devoted to your ugly and wrinkled friend." Gable joined him in his laughter.

"There are no sorrows or ailments within the boundaries of our imaginations, and that's where I dwell most of the time. Want to borrow the flute of my imagination, Fabian, you would become the master of health."

"With such worthy sentiments, Gable, you could be dubbed as the saint of the epicureans." Fabian's humor was getting ragged. "Cheer up, Ethel, for the sake of Kimberly, if not—"

His thoughts were disrupted by the sound of the doorbell.

Kimberly jumped to her feet as if startled, racing out of the room to answer the doorbell. A curtain of silence was lowered over all in her absence, but she returned soon, followed by Bryan.

"I don't recall inviting you!" Fabian dared not let go of his frayed humor, indicating a seat to Bryan.

"This simpleton never cares about invitations. An unwelcome guest wherever he goes," Bryan retorted, pulling a chair for himself, and greeting cheerfully.

"Don't mind Fabian, Bryan, his manners have gone sabbatical." Ethel's wit was coming to her rescue.

"Thank you, Ethel. Your warm, generous heart washes away the sin of Fabian's discourtesy. Besides, I have the honor of sitting with a celebrity."

"The honor is all mine since I never fail to admire the simpletons," Gable quipped, trying his best to still his pain, his heart pleading with Ethel, not Fabian.

"Come, Kimberly, get another plate," Ethel coaxed this time.

"Please, no. I've had my dinner." Bryan interceded quickly.

"Mom, are you still dropping off me at Tina's or should I take your car?" Kimberly asked.

"Oh, dear, it slipped my mind." Ethel heaved herself up, apologizing.

"In that case, we would sit in the living room." Fabian rose to his feet, Gable and Bryan following suit.

All three friends lodged comfortably in the living room were drinking coffee and engrossed in the idle pleasure of talking and laughing. Gable was participating mechanically. Fabian was unusually loud and caustic, teasing Bryan mostly and laughing artificially.

"Now that you're a bachelor again, don't you feel empty and lonesome? Not in love, the greatest tragedy, you would say." Fabian was intent on provoking Bryan to arguments.

"The levity of your expression, my friend, doesn't deserve a response, but I'm in a generous mood to oblige." Bryan chuckled. "Being in love is the greatest tragedy I'm more inclined to believe, for the time being, at least. The word love itself is empty and meaningless, as long as ego and selfishness rule our passions. But I don't want to delve into that, my pride is the cause of my loneliness and suffering, not the absence of love. Gloriously ignorant of my loneliness and suffering, I don't even know how I feel, only aware of a sharp affliction—the sense of pain, betrayal, bitterness."

"You hold on to your pride as the best of your virtues, Bryan," Gable commented with a sudden vehemence. "Slough it off and you'd be absolved of all afflictions."

"Yes, shred it to pieces," Fabian responded. "Be honest with your own self. Admit that you are lonely and suffering. Share your sense of pain and bitterness with your friends, a great therapy toward healing. We are friends, are we not?"

"Talking about friends, haven't seen Aslam and Heather in months, where are they?" Gable asked.

"Strangers, caught inside the whirlwind of their own rifts and prejudices, I should say," Bryan intoned thoughtfully. "The last time I saw Aslam he said, 'The absurdity of love is that it rises to its heights before dropping dead in its own throes of agony.'"

"Are you the victim of such absurdity too, Bryan?" Fabian goaded. "You look ghastly, if not ghostly," He added, oblivious to his own pallor.

"You yourself don't look like the picture of health, my friend," Bryan said.

"The reason behind that, Bryan, is physical, not emotional, and without the brand of absurdity," Gable expounded. "He's diagnosed with a cancer."

"Oh," Bryan murmured. "Hope, it's not that serious."

"If my guts don't revolt against the tyranny of such a corruption, I might yet live to suffer." Fabian laughed.

"How very noble to laugh at one's own sufferings. If I could do that I might be cured of my pain and loneliness," Bryan said solemnly.

"Besides pride, you are the victim of self-pity, Bryan," Gable said. "Your greed for pain is more than your longing to be *whole*. All sufferings vanish when a realization dawns upon the suffered that one clings to pain with the passion for gluttony and sense of gloating."

"You might as well be talking about you, Gable." Bryan's look was piercing. "Both of us suffer and know how to assuage our sufferings. You wash out yours in soapy suds of words, and I drown mine in sparkling drinks."

"Such dolts I have as friends," Fabian intoned. "I should be the one looking for a remedy to escape this curse of friendship."

"Baby dolts we are, if not the sinners, the noble brood of Adam and Eve." Bryan laughed.

"Don't fool yourself in tracing your heritage to the Garden of Eden. Monkeys are more likely your ancestors," Gable said jokingly.

"Children at heart and full-grown baboons, then. Darwin is my patron saint, and I his sinful disciple." Fabian's lightheartedness sounded artificial.

"How glorious this pain and hysteria." Bryan replied. "Can someone pound sense into our heads?"

"The sense and sanity, nothing makes sense, all empty and meaningless," Fabian said.

"No one here to pity the pitiful fools," Bryan said woefully.

"Absurdity of absurdities, verily I say unto you, is all absurdity." Gable sprang to his feet. "And with this absurd note as my talisman, I must be off." He strode out of the room, waving goodbye.

Time itself had left behind the embers of sixty-five days since Fabian's prognosis of cancer, and Gable had been unable to visit his friends, staying a prisoner to his own fever of torment and seclusion. This evening, tawny and mournful as ever, had startled him out of the jungle of his writing and he had decided to visit his friends. His car was racing down the familiar road and his thoughts receding in circles into the alleys of past. He had written feverishly for days, oblivious to the world around him, until Davie's sudden illness had startled him to *real awakening.* But right now, while wading through the marshlands of the past, his thoughts were empty and luminous. His mind was flashing a collage of scenes which were depicted in his novels.

The gods and goddess' were convening a grand meeting, priests and priestess' joining. The mists in his thoughts were conjuring witches and sorcerers. Vestal prostitutes were posing as virgins selling their chastity at the altars of lust and carnality. *Sister Fates* were there, too. Doom and death were hovering above, lowering shafts of pain, corrupting the breath of life. The graves of sins were torn open inside hearts, the pulse of life snuffed out, death still amorous and gluttonous.

Davie, Fabian. Are they both dying? I'm surely going mad. Gable's thoughts had come to an abrupt halt, much like his car careening into the driveway of Fabian's home.

"Fabian would be home soon." Ethel led Gable into the living room, her voice an echo of inner fear and anguish. "His chemotherapy lasts only an hour, and it has been two hours since he left home." She indicated the recliner to him, while wearily sinking into the cushiony depths of the couch.

"Where is Kimberly?" Gable asked.

"At her dancing lessons. She should be coming home soon, too." Ethel contrived a smile, noticing an anguished plea in Gable's eyes. "We remained friends, despite—" .

"The crumbs of our friendship are a feast to me, dear Ethel." Gable felt choked by his own passion, flaring inside him like a hurricane. "Forgive me. How is Fabian?"

"Suffering, I know. But he puts up a great façade, always smiling, never complaining," Ethel said with an abrupt vehemence, as if fighting her own pain and despair. "I wish he could groan or scream, to drain the cup of his agony, mental and physical. I'm exaggerating, perhaps, when with Kimberly, he is happy."

"You two look splendidly happy!" Fabian strode into the room unnoticed, absorbing the mournful expressions of his wife and friend.

"You look the same. Truly splendid." Gable sprang to his feet, searching the face of this man who had no resemblance to his friend Fabian.

"If splendid is the verdict, then let's celebrate." Fabian lowered himself beside Ethel. "How about a cup of coffee? Two, if Gable wishes to drink to my health."

"Lucky for you both the coffee pot is still on." Ethel rose slowly and thoughtfully.

"Where is Kimberly?" Fabian asked.

"At the dancing lessons," Ethel replied. "Completely forgot, I have to pick her up. Will get you coffee, and then leave." She hurried out of the room.

Both friends were silent after Ethel's hasty exit, their eyes locked, as if contemplating each other and wondering who was who under this armor of flesh and bones. Ethel returned quickly, carrying two mugs of coffee.

"I have your prescription with me. I'll have it filled on my way back," Ethel told Fabian after she served the coffee. "I am so glad Gable is here, I won't worry as much leaving you alone." She turned to Gable. "You would stay, I hope?"

"Until eternity," Gable replied.

"Don't worry, darling, Gable is a qualified babysitter, and I won't cause him any trouble."

"I am not so sure about you both, but I guess I have to trust." Ethel's departure was hurried.

"Wondering, how you stay so cheerful? Is the chemo helping?" Gable appeared to think aloud.

"At least, I don't have to get a haircut every month, the price is exorbitant." Fabian's mask of stoicism was breaking. "No cure to appease the pain but morphine. For the sake of Ethel and Kimberly, I go through chemo, knowing too well that it won't help, but they think it would save me somehow." He sipped his coffee, fighting the assault of nausea.

"You have to will wellness, Fabian," Gable began hopelessly. "Isn't pain a perception as well as well-being?"

"Much too real to be passed as a perception," Fabian confessed. "Mentally, I'm a glutton to pain, but physically, it gets intolerable."

"Stop being a glutton, my friend. If you can share half of your anguish with friends and family, you might be able to endure the physical suffering." Gable couldn't stand to look at the emaciated face of his friend, his eyes filled with pain.

"What would happen to Ethel, Kimberly, when I'm gone? Of course, it's useless to entertain such thoughts. Only their sadness' cut through my heart like knives, but then I console myself, nature has countless ways to heal and nourish." He gasped for breath.

"You must rest, Fabian. Close your eyes," Gable pleaded as he got to his feet and began pacing.

"Talk about your books, Gable. What new ideas are your characters parading these days?" Fabian asked, his eyes closing. "What are their views about life, the characters, I mean, whose lethal tongues sting as well as comfort?"

"Nothing new, Fabian." Gable lit a cigarette, resuming his pacing. "Life is a journey, as you said once, and we the nomads, stumbling along in this wild terrain of existence with a blind impulse to satisfy our needs, greeds, and passions. From the womb of death we are born, that's my own prosaic expression, living into the tomb of life, and longing to return to that mysterious *Womb* where something larger than life dwells, Bliss and immortality," he added.

"The protagonist in your last novel, if I recall correctly, holds fate in derision." Fabian said. "Do you believe in fate, Gable, or in God, to be more precise?"

"Not believing is a belief itself. Replacing belief with unbelief, one might argue, yet such arguments are the very foundations of confusion and bewilderment," Gable replied. "I dare not think about fate or God, for one blackens the page of my life, and the other rips my sanity to shreds."

"You'd be a perfect politician, Gable, wearing the art of dissimulation as your badge of honor," Fabian said, willing his pain to subside.

"Thanks for the compliment, Fabian. And I had flattered myself that I could easily become a preacher, if not a hermit, depending upon my mood." Gable paused, becoming aware of the blaze of agony in the eyes of his friend.

"I could be a preacher, Gable." Fabian was not succeeding in dispelling the fresh assault of pain. "I think of God so often now, since death is approaching closer."

"You must rest, Fabian, you're in pain." Gable lowered himself into a chair opposite Fabian.

Fabian murmured something, but his eyes were already closed, a subtle flush lending his cheeks the false glow of health. Gable absorbed the silence and sadness. The life with all its pain and struggle was stretched before his sight like a terrible canvas shuddering against the shadows of fate and inevitability. *The brushstrokes of the Artist Unknown on this canvas were shining like scarlet wounds, revealing the color of loss and tragedy, of death and annihilation, of bliss and union, the circles of unity dancing, dancing the dance of life and death.* So completely absorbed was he in contemplating this *canvas of existence* that he noticed neither Fabian's mute scrutiny, nor the arrival of Ethel and Kimberly.

"Hello, Uncle, you're not allowed to sleep in the chair." Kimberly flew into Gable's arms before he could stumble to his feet.

"How are you, Fabian, did you miss me?" Ethel stood watching her husband, while Kimberly clung to Gable as if she had not seen him in years.

"Terribly, my dear." Fabian smiled, averting his gaze to his daughter.

"I must have slept for an hour, it seems." Gable was laughing, turning to face his friends. "Well, my baby-sitting job is accomplished successfully, now I must go and nurse my bruised scripts." He waved farewell.

"Think of your friend's bruised health, too, and come often to bandage it." Fabian waved with an attempt at cheerfulness.

The evening sky with its saffron steaks was Gable's companion as he drove home. His own thoughts were carving wounds, bled white of all sorrow and as large as the void of loneliness pervading his soul and psyche. He could feel the breath of painful memories, all sprouting forth in his head like the tentacles of torture, twisted and gnarled, licking and flaming. One flame of love inside him, his own love unforgotten and unforgettable, was curling its tongue of fire. *Ethel, beloved.* Oblivious to his own thoughts he found himself in the familiar parlor.

"Are you ill, Gable?" Davie exclaimed. "Looks like you're hounded by robbers and cut-throats?"

"I'm fine, Davie," Gable responded. "Just feeling wretchedly and pugnaciously alive."

"You are ill, Gable," Davie muttered. "Look at you, a corpse in the morgue would look more alive than you do. I might look half dead to you, but the reason behind my state is my illness, what's yours?"

"His cankerous thoughts, nibbling at the very roots of his sanity when he can't spill them over the mounds of paper," Phoebe said.

"Darling." Davie's very eyes were flashing reproof.

"Fabian is dying, he has cancer. Goodnight." His feet were guiding him toward his own bedroom.

Twenty-Four ~ Fabian's Death

The reek of sin and gloom hung in the air, thick and palpitating, as Gable paced in his room like the one demented. He was oblivious to the peace and serenity of the early afternoon, unseeing the gold in sunshine which was flooding his room in bright rivulets. His heart was dark, muddied by the corruption of lust and grief—the *master* of its own *tyranny* he could neither fight, nor challenge. The victim of his own pain and loneliness, he was driven toward lust like one moth to a flame, his soul scorched and disfigured, relinquishing not its hold on body and mind, and avenging its own injuries by roasting both—the body and mind, into the fires of the damned. Phoebe, the flower of his lust and hate, was with him as he kept pacing, but his thoughts were licking the soot of guilt and grief.

Fever and restlessness were Gable's companions this afternoon, something inside him snapping and smoldering. He could feel the venom of his own kisses on Phoebe's lips, the concupiscence of last night coiling inside him like a serpent, one ugly heap of horror and disgust. His thoughts were fleeing this lump of deformity, knocking at the portals of fear and grief instead. Davie was there, suffering the nameless affliction of lung infection, his life and energy draining away slowly and gradually. Fabian was lying in the hospital, crawling towards the gate of death. Shame and tragedy were wrestling to win the wager of love inside the whirlwind of Gable's delirium, his thoughts summoning Bryan, then colliding headlong with Aslam and his family. Aslam's children were trooping down the street somewhere, *the little Jesuits* as Aslam called them. One pang of agony was screaming in Gable's head, goading him to go to the hospital, to visit his friend, holding the whip of discipline. His feet were obeying the command of agony, but before he could take another step, the she-devil had materialized before him as the *Queen of Nemesis*.

"You are going to kill yourself, Gable, by shutting yourself off in your room all the time. And pacing, if not writing." Phoebe flung herself upon the crumpled bed, pouting her lips voluptuously. "Are you really worried about your friend, Fabian, I mean, or thinking more about your *friend* Ethel, your beloved, your true love?"

"You would never understand the meaning of true love, my evil temptress." Gable's look was feverish and incisive. "Tempt me no more to sin, go away."

"You are a fool, Gable. An absolute fool to reject my love." Phoebe scoffed. "Your love for Ethel is a delusion, don't you know that? Why can't you forget her?"

"Sin and lust are not love, Phoebe, you have succeeded in burying me alive inside the volcano of my own guilt and grief." Gable murmured deliriously, resuming his pacing. "What do you know about love?"

"More than you do, my sinful lover." Phoebe laughed seductively. "At least, I absolve your sin with the gifts of joy and sweetness, which is me, each fiber in my flesh—since you tell me I have no soul, singing that love is not ever sinful."

"How I loathe you and myself." Gable pounced upon her with the fury of a man possessed, sealing her lips with kisses. "Now leave, before I kill you." He panted with rage and disgust. "I have to go and see my sick friend."

The canker of sickness was in Gable's heart as he sat visiting Fabian in the hospital. Pale and emaciated, Fabian tried to be brave, sucking back the mists of pain and attempting thin smiles. Gable's own features were pale, his look feverish, reaching out to the tall cedars through the window, but unseeing the glory of sunshine, polishing the leaves and verdure in nuances of jade and silver.

"What does one say when visiting a friend in the hospital?" Gable attempted to wade through the ocean of discomforting silence with this thoughtless comment. "Isn't it silly to ask how you're feeling? Knowing, that you are suffering?"

"The one and only topic of conversation around here, from room to room and floor to floor." Fabian smiled. "As to your indirect question about my health, I'm feeling comfortable, as if … as if the pain has decided to leave for good."

"This is wonderful, Fabian," Gable said with a dint of hope and cheerfulness. "Ethel's prayers are answered, I am sure."

"Don't you think I'm deceiving myself?" Fabian began hastily. "Something inside me is goading me to talk, about what, I don't know. What's the reason behind this greed to live? What sense in living?"

"All talk is senseless, Fabian," Gable replied. "And the reason for living, if any, or greed as you call it, doesn't make any sense, either. All these imponderables and yet talking is the symphony of existence, finding fulfillment in pain and pleasure. You're in a mood to talk, I can tell from the look in your eyes, Fabian. Go ahead, spill your heart out."

"Your pessimism is heartwarming, Gable." Fabian succeeded in eliciting one small laugh. "I have this need to talk, yes. No profundities, only simple, senseless talk, just for the sake of talking. This bridge of pain over the waters of life and death is my anchor, a sort of lighthouse against darkness, to observe and discern. I see more than what is visible to the naked eye, this tapestry of color in the world, dreamy and awesome. Flowers, flowers, now that they are my companions in my sick room. I study them as I have never studied them before. These tender, scented blooms of nature. Who is their Architect? When I look out of this slanting window, the grass down there assumes the texture of lace. And yet each blade of grass stares back at me, proud of its strength and fecundity, of its rebirth and invulnerability. Oh, the sound of the falling of the rain, a beautiful symphony. And yet this pain surfaces again and again, drowning all music and beauty. This scented living is not for mankind. The legacy of nature is not ours, no promise of rebirth or renewal. Only pain, doom, suffering, nothing but pain and—" He couldn't continue, noticing the arrival of the nurse.

"A couple of bullets to shoot the pain down." The nurse beamed, holding out yellow pills and a glass of water.

"Even when there is no pain," Fabian quipped before swallowing the pills.

"That nurse is a bullet herself," Gable commented after the nurse flitted out of the room as breezily as she had entered. "You must rest now, Fabian."

"I can't rest, Gable, not until I'm done saying what I have to say," Fabian began hastily. "So many things crowding in my head and my thoughts are muddled. Kimberly, she is in love, but I wish I can see her married before I die. And Ethel, how would she live—alone? I have a confession to make, my guilt— a secret and a promise from you. You must remember and fulfill this promise ...." He couldn't finish, choked by his emotions and a fit of coughing.

"You must rest, Fabian. Not another word. I 'll be back tomorrow, you can tell me then. You're tired, close your eyes."

"I must say what I have to say, Gable. Don't leave me yet, or I won't be able to say it. You have always been in love with Ethel, you will always be that way, it can't be denied," Fabian declared. "I had acted wickedly stealing your love from you. Forgive, forgive. Hold sacred my last wish. Marry her when I'm gone. Promise, and then I will die in peace."

Gable stood, stunned, unable to stir or speak. His lips moved to form words, but no sound issued forth, only his thoughts clamoring a litany of prayers. An eternity slipped past as the two friends watched each other in silence. This curtain of silence was broken by the sudden appearance of Ethel.

"Darling," Fabian could barely speak, his look glazed.

"Ethel," Gable said, "sorry, I must be on my way. Will see you to-morrow."

"No, you can't leave, Gable," Fabian cried with a sudden vehe-mence, his eyes blazing. "Not until you witness what I have to say to Ethel." He was holding his wife captive in his feverish gaze. "First, my dear, could you ever forgive me? But that doesn't matter, promise me, you will marry Gable."

Gable was already out of the room, stumbling down the staircase, his thoughts one hoary conflagration. He could feel the crackle of his thoughts in conformity with his reckless driving. Frenzy and despair were rising inside him like a fever on the verge of nausea. The festering wound of love deep within him was bleeding, spewing forth the abscess of pain. This blind, raging violence inside the very fabric of his psyche was stilled with an abrupt, astonishing sense of peace and sadness. He could see the reeds of hope swaying merrily, polished by the light of love and forgiveness. Fabian was no more, effaced by the wand of fates. Ethel was emerging forth as Venus, radiant and unapproachable. An overwhelming sense of grief was his companion, blinding his sight and senses, as he stumbled into the house, racing up the staircase. Shooting straight for his room, he almost collided with Phoebe, who blocked his way like a vile temptress.

"You look ill, Gable," Phoebe' said. "What's wrong? Don't just stand there, say something. Even your burst of mockery would be welcome. I didn't think I'd ever say that."

"Fabian is dying." Gable could hear his own low moan.

"How very convenient," Phoebe chanted. "Your flimsy grief and your mighty love for Ethel. You are hoping you would—"

"The reek of your thoughts corrupts the very name of love on your lips, Phoebe," Gable cried suddenly, rage and disgust blazing in his heart. "Next time you cross my path, make sure your pretty throat is well protected."

**

Another fury, another time, were gouged solid in Gable's head as he sat in his study, writing feverishly, rather belligerently. Four long months since Fabian's death and the specks of grief inside him were alive, pulsating with the rhythm of pain and renewal in death and in loss. Day after day he had sat with Ethel, sharing her grief and his own sadness, the rivers of passion inside him blocked and churning. Now, his head was heavy, the autumnal evening whimpering through the open windows. He could hear the frolic in the wind and rustling of the leaves, his thoughts peering tremulously into the eyes of future where Davie's whole being could be seen afflicted with pain and disease. Gable closed his eyes, daring not to name the nameless illness, manifesting in languor and loss of appetite. His thoughts were forcing their way out of fear which had become their permanent abode since the death of Fabian. Something inside him was groping for light, fleeing hopelessness and falling right into the pit of helplessness.

Why can't I get down on my knees and ask for the crumbs of love from Ethel? Why don't I ask her to marry me? Gable's heart sank at the sudden assault of his sin and insanity.

Suddenly, Phoebe, the she-devil was a looming threat over his shoulders, his heart cringing with fear and shame. One wisp of a realization was dawning upon him that she was unwell, had grown aloof, as if plotting and scheming. She hadn't forced her sinful lust upon him for the past four months, permitting him the leisure of daily visits to Ethel, only greeting him with a pale, mysterious smile in the presence of Davie. An abrupt, overwhelming sense of fatigue and sorrow were enveloping Gable's whole being into mists dark and turbulent. He could feel the presence of Phoebe in this room and the odor of his own sin. The witchcraft of his thoughts was snatched into the rude hands of reality as Phoebe sailed toward him, robed in her much-too familiar wicked apparel.

"A paragon of health and exuberance once again," Gable commented, fear clutching his heart and soul.

"You don't look too bad, either. Ironic, isn't it, Gable, that despite pain and grief over the loss of your dear, dear friend, you are looking much better than when I saw you the very first time."

"Should I congratulate you on your choice of words, Phoebe?" Gable watched her thoughtfully. "You wouldn't understand the concept of irony even if it hit you on the head."

"Do you think you can marry Ethel, Gable, now that Fabian is dead?" Phoebe challenged. "No, that can never be as long as I live. You are chained to me forever and will never be free."

"I was never chained to you, Phoebe. I'm the victim of my own lust and of your wickedness," Gable replied, as if to himself. "The chains of my sin are rusted and broken. Only the weight of guilt and penance is my cross to seek peace and forgiveness."

"Don't deceive yourself, Gable. You will love me always. You will never be free." Phoebe laughed.

"Sick. Demented, you are, Phoebe. What makes you think that you have the power to make me wallow into this river of sin forever?" Gable began to pace, delirium clouding his thoughts. "Would you cast a spell over me, seducing me in my sleep?"

"No spell, you fool," Phoebe chanted. "If you spurn my love, I would tell Davie about our sinful relationship, even to the very last details scented with passion and madness."

"The reek of sin." Gable went to the window, his back towards her. "No, you wouldn't. Davie would die of grief," he uttered.

"Do you think I care, Gable? Forget about Ethel, Gable, I would never let you go."

"You would not dare hurt Davie? How could you?" Gable swung around to face her. "Yes, you would. What do you want from me?"

"Don't look so stricken, love," Phoebe mocked. "Come, kiss me, and all would be forgotten."

"One little kiss, Phoebe?" Gable said in defeat. "Your hunger for passions foul and sinful can never be slaked with one kiss." He began to pace again, crushed under the burden of his grief and guilt.

"You are right, Gable." Phoebe laughed hysterically. "I want to be kissed again and again and forever. Anytime of the night or day, whenever I want."

"Go away, you ...." The word *slut* was choked inside the very pools of Gable's rage and anguish. "If it were not for Davie, I would kill you right this moment."

"I love you, Gable," Phoebe whispered sweetly.

"Love is not a commodity you can purchase in this glittering bazaar of a world, brimming with lust and greed," Gable yelled, his anger flaring. "Love is a spirit free and boundless, not a *thing* one can beg, borrow or steal."

"I am not begging, Gable, I'm demanding. You must love me, if you care to save your little brother from the agony of grief."

"You." Gable stumbled before standing before her like the one doomed.

"Kill me, if that is what you desire the most?" Phoebe challenged.

"The murderous streak in me is compelling me to do violence, Phoebe, go away." Gable could barely speak.

"You leave me no choice, but the sheer delight of confession, then." Phoebe began to leave.

"Tortures of the damned." Gable snatched her fiercely into his arms, kissing and hurting her with the violence of his hatred and madness.

***

The tides of time and torture were swallowed into one solid year, and Gable was gulfs apart from his beloved as he had been since the death of Fabian. He was driving on the familiar road toward Ethel's home, his heart aching and lonesome. The early spring, scented with hopes, was his companion, yet his heart was a cauldron of hopelessness. Deep within him were the marshlands of anguish where Davie lay ill and suffering, getting closer to death, yet clinging to life. But his thoughts dared not look into those depths, striving toward hope and defying the edict of fate. His thoughts were holding sacred the dying wish of his friend, the holy promise in love and marriage, such holiness corrupted by his sin. *You can't marry Ethel. You can't hurt Davie. You will remain the slave of she-devil.*

"I was hoping you'd come." Ethel waved from the porch, her smile fading as soon as she noticed the stark anguish in his eyes. "Let's sit in the garden, apple blossoms are lovely." She dragged him along toward the bench, making him sit beside her. "Something has been eating you inside out. Look at you. Rivers of pain in your eyes. No use asking, I guess, keeping your pain buried inside you. God knows, I've tried, and I know you are hurting, but you won't tell."

"I am not hurting, Ethel. No, I'm not," Gable protested, eliciting one of his boyish smiles reserved only for his beloved. "No pain, only a curse. Can't contain all this happiness of sitting with you. I think I'm afraid of happiness, afraid of losing it. In my thoughts I know no such fear, talking with you and laughing. Yes, in my thoughts, you are closer to me than reality. And yet, I can't endure this gulf of separation between us, and my pain, and my curse." He claimed her hand, pressing it into his own most gently.

"A poet and a dreamer, Gable, you have always been like that," Ethel said thoughtfully. "You have really not lived, only in dreams, shutting off you pain, rather nurturing it."

"A dreamer, yes, dear Ethel." Gable looked into her eyes. "In my dreams, you are a *star*. Pure, white, brilliant. A dazzling star. I love you, Ethel, I always have, and I always will. I wish, I mean, I'm unworthy, even to hope. This curse. Maybe, one day, I would have the courage to tell you all, ready for anything, of your anger or punishment, hoping for mercy—forgiveness, most of all."

"Didn't you forgive me, Gable? My hasty marriage to Fabian? Don't you think I'm capable of forgiving, and for what? Well, let's talk of something cheerful. Kimberly is getting married in a couple of months, and you would have the honor of giving the bride away. I would miss her of course. This big house, wonder, if I would be lonely."

"Kimberly. You ...."

"What's wrong, Gable?"

"Nothing, my love." Gable couldn't help stifling one groan. "I want to be with you, always. Whether you need me or not. But I can't, it hurts. I'm frightened. A coward, perhaps, and a sinner."

"What do you fear, Gable? Can't understand this agony in your—"

"My sweet sadness." Gable crushed her into his arms with a sudden violence. "Forgive me, love." He relaxed his grip, holding her gently. "This fear I must fight alone. I must leave. Tomorrow, yes, tomorrow, I will be in a better frame of mind. Pray for me." He released her, fleeing toward his car as if pursued by the demons.

Ethel couldn't move. She closed her eyes as if blocking out the portrait of sorrow, which was Gable, professing love, guarding fear, and fleeing. *From what?* She could hear the grinding of wheels on the gravel, her own heart pounded to dust and soot.

You and Gable have not ever stopped loving each other— must marry, this plea from Fabian's lips on his deathbed was painful gong.

A spray of apple blossoms, rocked by the caprice of the wind, were teasing Ethel's cheeks. The pulse of pain and loneliness within her was awakening, seeking, seeking—oblivion.

Twenty-Five ~ Tortures of the Damned

The sky was a torrent of tears as Gable paced in his room, trying to discipline his anguished thoughts to some semblance of peace before he could visit Ethel. His thoughts were not complying, racing down the rungs of past six months, and getting lost into the pools of sadness. Kimberly was married, leaving behind a void inside the heart of her mother, but visiting her as often as he himself did, with much longing and anticipation. The mere thought of Davie's illness shot a spasm of pain through his whole frame like a bolt of lightning. Davie's illness, nameless and unidentified, sapped his brother's strength and caused much suffering.

Davie is dying — no. I'm dying. Waiting, waiting for what? Why can't I tell Ethel? Gable's thoughts were wallowing inside the muddied waters of his sin and bondage. *Was Eve the bane of Adam? Was Cain the foe of Abel?* He was forcing his thoughts back to the lighthearted gaiety at Kimberly's wedding.

Bryan was at the wedding, happy as he claimed to be, after his divorce, then doling out his bulletin of news with his usual passion for gossip and entertainment. Aslam had packed his bags and was settled in London, his British-born wife, Heather, happy with her family. Their American-born children resisted this move, but since the clouds of litigation hung low over Aslam's shoulders by a disgruntled patient, he was fortunate to leave the U.S. along with his family.

Eternity itself rests in unity, and this image we call time. This epigram of Plato, quoted by Bryan, was surfacing in Gable's head once again, but he was fleeing his thoughts as well as his room.

Gable could hear the whistling of wind inside his car, his windshield wipers working to keep up with the downpour. His mind was churning inanities as he found himself parked amidst the floodgates of a driveway which had become his holy shrine to be visited religiously.

Is it wicked to love? Are hopes evil? Can pure longings be sinful? Gable was rushing out of his car without thinking, and straight for the front doors.

"Oh, Gable." Ethel let him in with a cry of delight. "Let me fetch a towel." She scurried toward the bathroom.

Gable stood shivering, daring not to move lest he drag the pool of water along with him onto the carpet. Ethel returned with a towel, holding it out and laughing to herself.

"Now dry yourself before you catch cold," Ethel admonished with a little toss of her head. "What made you venture out in such beastly weather?" She beckoned him to the living-room.

"You, my love," Gable said, drying his hair vigorously. "You sound much like Heather. I was thinking about Aslam and Heather this afternoon."

"You should be ashamed of yourself, Gable. Here, let me see. You have a fever. You're ill." Ethel touched his brow, then made him sit beside her.

"No. I am perfectly well," Gable said with unusual vehemence. "Beloved. My one and only beloved. My gentle sadness. Could you ever forgive me? I've neglected visiting you—my shrine. Davie has been ill, and I have been trying too ..." He couldn't continue, becoming aware of fear in Ethel's eyes and of his own rambling.

"You must see a doctor, Gable," Ethel coaxed. "For my sake, for the sake of Davie."

"For your sake alone, my precious one. Forgive. Yes, I'm not well. How is Kimberly?"

"Happy." Ethel was trying her best to choke her fears. "She's visiting next Friday. You can't join us unless you promise to see a doctor and get some rest."

"Your slave, my love, I will do that right now." Gable snatched her hands into his own, kissing them feverishly. Then he fled.

Gable, enveloped in the stupor of his dreams and delirium, could hear the hammering in his head and inside his heart. His lips were parched, and each muscle in his body aching. He stirred, moaning feebly, trying to open his eyes. Once his heavy eyelids were fluttered open, he could see himself tucked under clean sheets in his own bed, in his own room. His bedside table was cluttered with bottles of medicines. Before he could close his eyes, his sight alighted on Davie, who sat dozing in his wheel-chair.

"Davie," Gable uttered.

"I'm with you, Gable. Don't say a word, rest." Davie opened his eyes, his pallor intensified by the dark circles under his eyes.

"Davie." Gable jerked himself up to a sitting position, stifling a groan. "How long I have been lying here? Where do all these medicines come from?"

"You were ill, Gable, raving." Davie's lips trembled, though his voice was controlled. "Your need rest—nourishment. Phoebe should be bringing you hot soup, she's fixing it herself."

"You're in pain, Davie, I can tell. You should be in bed. It seems like I've been lying in here for years. How long you have been sitting here? All these medicines, I don't recall going to a doctor."

"All night you have been rambling, Gable, feverish and delirious. My personal physician was kind enough to make a house call. Phoebe and I have been shooting these pills down your throat. Great help, these pills, to bring your fever down."

"You better eat this soup, Gable, if you want to get well." Phoebe held out the bowl of soup to him. "Next time you decide to soak yourself in rain, make sure to pay your respects to your doctor before you get home."

"Darling," Davie said in a tone of reproof.

"All my fault, Davie, that's true, I deserve it." Gable swallowed a spoonful, his voice choked by a flood of contrition.

"After you finish eating, Gable, you need to close your eyes and rest, whether you deserve it or not," Davie said, wheeling his chair away. "Phoebe will try her best to lull me to sleep, or to stupor, whichever comes first." He was aiming for the door, Phoebe plodding behind his chair.

***

Fever and sickness were in Gable's head, though he pretended to be whole and healthy. He caressed the familiar road wending its way toward the home of his Beloved. Abandoned on the front seat was a bouquet of red roses he had no recollection of purchasing, his thoughts immersed deep into a week-long agony of recovery. He was feeling strong and in control, though the ravages of illness were visible on his pale, gaunt features. The raw wound of ache and loneliness within him was throbbing, clinging to Davie with prayers and supplications. Davie was bed-ridden, cradled into the haze of morphine. Smiling, always smiling.

If you truly wish to pray for my health, Gable, pray — do not barter your own. This comment of Davie was a fresh stab to Gable's awareness as he parked his car. Scarlet his wounds, much like the brilliant bouquet in his arms, were wafting their own scent of pain as he rushed out to meet his beloved.

"How lovely, and they smell so good." Ethel claimed the bouquet with squeals of delight. "I would spend half the night arranging them, I'm sure." She flitted out of the room to put the roses in water.

"My sweet flower." Gable snatched Ethel into one eager embrace as soon as she returned. "Flowers, my love, remind me of weddings and funerals both, such irony of life. Forgive me, love, I've frightened you." He released her gently.

"Gable, you are still not well. You didn't go to the doctor?"

"I did, dear Ethel, I did," Gable replied. "I've been swallowing more pills than food. "Won't you offer me a seat?" He stumbled toward the sofa.

"I would urge you to lie down, you look ill." Ethel gasped for breath. "Why didn't I notice that before?"

"Please sit with me," Gable pleaded. "Each moment away from you stabs me with the splinter of agony." He claimed her hand as she lowered herself beside him. "Forgive me, for suffering thus … for loving—"

"Love is pure joy, seeking not forgiveness, but fulfillment." Ethel averted her eyes.

"For suffering then, can one seek forgiveness?" Gable asked.

"I know, you suffer, Gable. But why?"

"I wish I can tell you all. To share all. To lay bare my soul. My foul, sinful soul. To ask your forgiveness. But I fear you would never forgive me. You would never want to see me again. I cannot bear even the thought of losing you again."

"You are ill, Gable. You have no cause to fear," Ethel replied.

"Beloved." Gable could barely stifle a groan. "I would write down my sins, for you to read. To judge—to forgive, if you can."

"Hush, Gable, don't say another word," Ethel cried suddenly. "If it is any consolation to you, I forgive you completely and absolutely. For what, only God knows, but I do forgive. Let's have some coffee and forget about all this talk of sin and forgiveness. May I have my hand back?" She stood, her hand still clutched by Gable.

"May I keep it?" Gable smiled, urging her to sit down. "We would have coffee, later."

"Tylenol then, you feel feverish." Ethel elicited a smile. "You said you went to the doctor, what did he say?"

"Nothing. He came to our house, I don't even know when. I was delirious. Left jars of pills, it seems, I 've been swallowing them since then. I'm not ill, it's only madness. Madness of being madly in love with you. My sweet sadness, I bring you nothing but unhappiness. Yet, I can't help seeing you. You are a balm to my madness, my only link to sanity. My life, my soul."

"Why don't you let me cure your madness then, Gable?" Ethel appealed. "Why must you suffer? Why not share your pains and sorrows, your sins and fears, if that's what you think they are?"

"I would, my love, I would," Gable repeated passionately. "Could you suffer the imbecile in me a little longer 'til I am able blacken the pages with my sins. Fear is not the only reason which keeps me away from doing just that, but the doom and gloom of Davie's health, declining rapidly. He's suffering, smiling away the pain and stupor."

"Sorry. Is he in much pain? Does the medication help? I didn't know he was that ill," Ethel said rather than asked.

"Morphine, the panacea for all suffering, I guess."

"Davie needs you, Gable. You must stay with him, instead of, well …." Ethel's thoughts were caught into a hurricane of discoveries as if she was about to land upon the mystery of Gable's pain and madness. "I'll come and visit you every day if you want, but you must stay with him and tend to his needs."

"Davie would be pleased, and I, of course, would be eternally grateful."

"Phoebe, poor girl, her sufferings must be great," Ethel demurred aloud.

"That vixen." Gable leaped to his feet as if stung. "Forgive me, love, I would explain this later. Much sooner, at the peril of my own loss and grief." He turned, fighting his need, desire to hold her into his arms. "No, I must not repeat my sins." He fled.

Twenty-Six ~ Mating of Souls

A sad glow from sunset in hues of mauve and carmine was accentuating Gable's pallor as he sat at his desk absorbed in writing. The strokes of his pen were bold, his fingers working feverishly, spilling the fire of his sins. Four tortured months of loss and grief had glided past since Davie's death, and he was still suspended in the limbo of agony and indecision. Ethel was with him, it seemed, guiding his hand, licking away his pain and despair, but his thoughts for some strange, astonishing reason were communing with Bryan, who had showed up two months after the death of Davie.

Pain is the breath of life. Bryan had chanted histrionically. *Pain is fire and ether, licking wounds inside the hearts, carving its way into the rivulets of souls, and kindling a bonfire of passions — hopes, longings, burning forever, smoldering eternally.*

Gable's fingers came to a sudden halt, his hands pressing the tablets of his sins into neat folds and slipping them into a white envelope. His lips were trembling as he licked the envelope before sealing it, a hurricane of grief clamping his heart into pincers of agony and hopelessness.

A thinking, breathing, suffering dolt I am. The pain of love inside him was a large rent, a bleeding, whimpering laceration. His eyes settled on the neglected page of his unfinished villanelle. Involuntarily, his hands were reaching out, his fingers moving to touch the hem of finality.

Roots of death in illusions have learnt to array
The naked dreams in raiments of lies on life's tree
Let me sleep in peace, wake me up on Judgment Day
All thoughts are dunes of sand and mind a pot of clay

Gable couldn't finish the line. Phoebe sailed into the room, wafting the scent of hauteur and concupiscence.

"Look at you, how extravagantly you are dressed," Phoebe sang most charmingly. "Isn't it ridiculous to dress that way, even if one has a dinner engagement?"

"Not, if one is eager to propose to his beloved," Gable said without acknowledging her presence.

"The inevitable which would never happen. Could you take me out to dinner, just this once, in remembrance of Davie?" Her voice was choked.

"How naïve you are, Phoebe, not ever afraid, even to play harlot with your own passions." Gable eased himself up, the flood of pity and sadness in his eyes a shuddering ocean. "I'm sorry."

"You cannot leave, Gable, you cannot. I won't let you," Phoebe cried.

"How would you make me stay?" Gable said, his look sad and gentle.

"I would kill myself, if you leave. Without you, I cannot live. Kiss me, Gable, please."

Davie would be happy to see you up there. Gable said to himself. "Maybe, you would learn to be faithful to him in that part of the world? You don't love anyone, Phoebe, but your own vanity and wickedness. I, on the other hand, though wallowing into my own sin and follies, have always loved Ethel, will always love her. Want to marry her, if she will have me."

"I have a pre-nuptial gift for your precious bride, Gable." Phoebe laughed. "My wedding present to her would be a letter, titled, *adultery*."

"Paradoxically, Phoebe, my gift to her matches yours. But she would receive mine first." He marched out, leaving behind the echo of his confession.

Driving home to beloved seemed like a holy, painful ritual to Gable this evening, as if the entire world stood still, awaiting the *hour of pilgrimage.* He was aware of the glorious sunset in his rearview mirror, a tapestry of colors, splashed with ocher and vermilion. His thoughts were a collage of colors, the purity of his youth surfacing, holding out the beacon of his love for Ethel alone. All follies of the past were fading somewhere inside the cauldron of loss, grief, madness. More colors were bleeding out of *color*, all colors swallowed by the mists of agony in death. Hope was a shining mirage, yet undulating with the pulse of time, more real than sunsets or thoughts. Gable had reached the familiar home—his haven. He had turned the ignition off, his thoughts throwing open the gates of Eden, but he was a stranger in there, bewildered, shuddering. He had no idea when he had left his car or how he was transported into the living room. Much like magic, the fabric of reality was grazing his awareness as an emblem of revelation. Ethel was seated on the sofa, the primrose-blue in her eyes vivid and sparkling.

"My love." Gable's knees were buckling under him, as he kneeled, touching Ethel's feet, his head into her lap. "This sinner before you is pleading forgiveness. Forgive me if you can, punish me if you will, and pity, if not love. Would you marry me, Ethel?"

"Yes, Gable, yes." Ethel said, stroking his hair, her heart singing the hymns of love ineffable and love unforgotten.

"Beloved." Gable stumbled to his feet, delirious and bewildered. "Hoping beyond hope that you change not your mind when my sins are revealed to you." He snatched the letter out of his pocked, holding it out to her. "I will wait until you have read each word of my character so foul and corrupt."

"Gable," Ethel said softly, claiming the letter reluctantly, "may I have a cigarette?" .

"You need a shot of whiskey, not a cigarette, my Love. The only time I've seen you smoking was when you learned that I was to be sent to prison." He held out the light to her.

"And that was the last time, Gable." Ethel snatched the lighter, its flame licking the white envelope in her hands. "I have fed your sins to the flames, Gable." She was quick to reach the hearth, tossing the burning sins into the heart of the fireplace. "Yes, yes, a thousand times, yes. I will marry you." She fell weeping into the arms of Gable, both caressed by the mists of sublime bliss.

Let me sleep in peace, wake me up on Judgment Day
My wearied and restless soul cries in plea
All thoughts are dunes of sand, and mind a pot of clay
Sorrows weep no more, aged grief has turned all gray
Negation in nothingness dares to flee
All thoughts are dunes of sand, and mind a pot of clay
Spirit of agony has lost its power to slay
The embittered heart in torments of glee
All thoughts are dunes of sand, and mind a pot of clay

Surcease has trodden all paths to pave the way
Into the chambers of hope where blindness can see
All thoughts are dunes of sand, and mind a pot of clay
Lost youth at the altars of ruins need not pray
The nemesis silent, sealed by God's holy decree
All thoughts are dunes of sand, and mind a pot of clay
Roots of death in illusions have learnt to array
The naked dreams in raiments of lies on life's tree
Let me sleep in peace, wake me up on Judgment Day
All thoughts are dunes of sand, and mind a pot of clay

About the Author

Farzana Moon is a poet, historian and a playwright. Writes Sufi poetry, historical, biographical accounts of the Moghul emperors and plays based on stories from religion and folklore. Her published works in religion and spirituality are: *Irem of the Crimson Desert; Sufis and Mystics of the World; Prophet Muhammad: The First Sufi of Islam; No Islam But Islam; Sharia Exposed.* Published works in the sequels of the Moghul emperors are: *Babur, The First Moghul In India; The Moghul Exile; Divine Akbar and Holy India; The Moghul Hedonist: Glorious Taj and Beloved Immortal; The Moghul Saint of Insanity; Poet Emperor of the Last of the Moghuls: Bahadur Shah Zafar.* Another of her published book in history is about the partition of India and Pakistan, Holocaust of the East. Her play *Osama The Demented* had a staged reading in Stockholm. Another of her play, *Russian Roulette*, is being considered for production. Her book, *The American Queen*, about the wife of Hazrat Inayat Khan, Ora Ray Baker who was born in Albuquerque, New Mexico USA is being considered for publication.

ALL THINGS THAT MATTER PRESS

FOR MORE INFORMATION ON TITLES AVAILABLE FROM
ALL THINGS THAT MATTER PRESS, GO TO
http://allthingsthatmatterpress.com
or contact us at
allthingsthatmatterpress@gmail.com

If you enjoyed this book, please post a review on Amazon.com and
your favorite social media sites.
Thank you!